Finding His Wa
Benson Brothers:

C000151166

J.P. Oliver & Linda Kandi

© 2019
Disclaimer

Contents

Chapter 1 - *Joshua*

I woke up to the sound of my own pulse and the aching feeling of my stomach, twisting in an effort to expel itself of poison.

I blinked, rapidly, ignoring the way my head pounded in unison with that blinking, and tried to get my bearings. Was I dying? Was this what it felt like to die?

Good God, how much had I drank last night?

Lying on the couch, I ignored the rolling wave of nausea that had woken me up from my sleep. The overhead light was still on from when I'd stumbled home yesterday, one of my shoes still tightly tied on my foot. I groaned loudly, and wiped my hands down my face. My mouth felt like sweaty cotton and tasted so much worse; my body was pulsing, as if it was taking extreme effort for my blood to circulate.

The ceiling fan spun in slow circles, the noise of the blades blaring loudly when my hangover mixed with the hot, summer heat of Kentucky. It was my own fault for staying out at Billiards so late last night—there were very few things that mixed worse than shots, beer, and end of college nostalgia.

As of yesterday, I was officially graduated from university. I had a bachelor's degree in marketing, a minor in public relations, and absolutely no job prospects. Last night, getting *smashed* with my friends seemed like a good idea. Today, alone in an apartment with a lease of about two more weeks, it felt like I was resigning myself to a life of exactly this: nauseous, alone, sitting on a couch.

I was basically homeless, unemployed, with no prospects, and all of my friends had gotten jobs in Louisville—I guessed I could go with them, try to find a small place and just any old job to pay the bills.

I groaned again.

This time, the sound echoed. I frowned, blinking up at the ceiling fan. The groaning kept going even after I'd closed my mouth.

With a nearly Herculean effort, I managed to get myself in the upright position.

Griffin Hill was sprawled across the floor, his arms and legs spread into a starfish as he groaned face down into my carpet. I laughed at him, only to stop once it made my head start to pound.

"Am I *dead*?" His muffled voice sounded distraught and too loud. "Please, oh, merciful God, let me be dead."

I grabbed the nearest object—thankfully for Griff, it was a soft throw pillow—and chucked it at him. It hit the back of his head and bounced off.

He froze. "God?"

"Fuck *off,* Griff." I threw another pillow.

Slowly, he rolled over, gasping at the effort. He was both pale and bright red at once, eyes bloodshot and face crinkled with the heaviness he'd been sleeping with. His hair looked matted to his skull. I winced and hoped I didn't look as bad as he did—I was sure I did.

"Did we drink *all* of the liquor last night?"

I nodded solemnly. "There's likely none left in the continental US."

He laughed and then grabbed his head, wincing.

Griff and I had been best friends since orientation freshman year. This was far from the first time we'd woken up in each other's apartment, hungover beyond belief.

We sat in comfortable, miserable silence for a few minutes. Griff's eyes were locked on the ceiling fan and I wondered if he was emotionally taking stock the way I had been a few minutes ago.

I didn't have it in me to be introspective at the moment; I was too busy trying to decide if food was the best idea I'd ever had or the beginning of the end for me.

After a few minutes, I landed on hunger.

"I would trade my life for a taco right now," I said, searching around for my other shoe.

Griffin's head lolled to the side and he stared at me.

Aha! It was under the coffee table. I took a deep breath to calm the nausea and then lowered myself from the couch, cursing softly as I stuck my arm under the table to grab my abandoned shoe.

Once appropriately put on my foot, I heaved myself up and to the bathroom. A quick glance in the mirror told me that I looked way worse than I could have imagined. My eyes were bloodshot, my hair standing nearly straight up, and I had a five o'clock shadow that was quickly nearing midnight. I shook my head, clenching my eyes shut, and counted to ten. Griff was making some sort of miserable noises outside of the door.

I washed my face, brushed my teeth twice, and eventually managed to leave the bathroom looking like I had been grazed by a truck, not fully hit by it. It was an improvement.

Griff sat with his back against the couch, his face twisted in concentration as he struggled to get his shoes on. I laughed and then winced at the way my head started to pulse.

"I'm never drinking again," Griff vowed, pointlessly.

It took us another twenty minutes to get to Joe's, our group's favorite diner. Griff went directly to the counter to get us coffee from Shelly.

"My girl," he called, voice decibels above what a hungover asshole should be willing to use. "Tell me that Shawn got his head out of his ass and took back that ugly cranberry sweater."

"Griff, you know he did not."

"I'll kill him!"

I tuned them out, groaning at the sounds of the restaurant. If Griff's loud voice was good for anything, though, it was befriending people and hopefully his rapport with Shelly would bring my food sooner. I slid into a booth and dropped my head into my hands, groaning.

Griff slid into the booth across from me and I quickly grabbed my coffee. "I ordered us two specials with extra hash browns."

The special had pancakes, eggs, bacon, and hash browns. It wasn't a taco but it would do.

"Thank God," I mumbled. The roof of my mouth was a little burnt from how quickly I was drinking my coffee, but the warm caffeine was already working its way through my system. I felt better already.

Griff looked like he had recently risen from the grave. He intermittently sipped his coffee and groaned.

"Can't believe this is the last time we'll be here, hungover, for the foreseeable future," he said.

I frowned. "I don't like that."

"Me, either," he leaned back, hands curled around his mug. Shelly came by and refilled our mugs while talking to another table. I waved, but more customers came through the door and she darted off.

"Have you found your studio space yet?"

Griff was an artist and, after putting his stuff in a few galleries around the university, was looking to open his own art gallery.

He shrugged. "I'm still working on getting the financing to come through. It's almost like banks *don't* want to support unemployed, young artists with no financial safety net?"

I laughed. "Wow, what dicks."

"Amen," he lifted his coffee and we clinked our mugs.

A new waiter came by and dropped off our plates, promising to be back with the extra hash browns soon.

"So if you're still working on financing, why are you leaving so soon?" I knew there was a distinct layer of *whine* in my voice, but I didn't want Griff to leave; I didn't want any of them to leave, at least not until I was leaving, too.

Griff's fork scraped across the plate, the sound blending into the faded hum of white noise in the restaurant. "Well, the financing isn't here—it's in the same city as the gallery space. So I'm going to move there, throw all my eggs in one basket, and, I don't know. Take up praying."

I had to admit that while it seemed objectively like a terrible plan, it was a very Griffin plan and he had a way of things working out well for him. I couldn't imagine anyone denying him, even if what he was asking for was a hell of lot of money.

Griff shoveled nearly a whole pancake in his mouth and then, jaw pushed open from the food, mumbled, "What are you going to do?"

I groaned and then followed his lead, shoving as much food as possible in my mouth to buy myself a few extra seconds of thought.

We chewed painstakingly slowly, trying to avoid choking and conversation.

"I don't have a job lined up and the apartment lease is over soon and I actually and literally have no idea what I am *doing*." There was an edge of panic under my tone, heightened by dehydration and caffeine.

"Go on a road trip!" he suggested.

"A road trip," I rolled my eyes. "Alone? To what destination?"

He stabbed a giant piece of egg and raised his fork threateningly. "Does it matter?"

I tilted my head. "What's the difference between going on an aimless road trip and living in my car?"

Griff popped the egg in his mouth, humming as he considered. His eyes widened and he started to talk so quickly that he choked on a bit of his food, grabbing at his coffee as he coughed.

I waited until his moment subsided, lifting my own mug to my lips.

"That DNA result stuff," he said, slapping his hand down on the table for emphasis. "That genome what-fuck we got you at Christmas."

The test results that gave me information on my birth family, relatives of the people whose genes I shared. I had been in foster care since before I could remember and after a truly embarrassing drunken night where I had confided a very deep desire to actually *meet* the people that had, well, sired me, my friends had all chipped in and paid for a DNA test.

The results, though opened and thoroughly memorized, had been sitting untouched on my desk for the last five months.

"What about it?"

"Go there," Griff suggested, shrugging one shoulder. "Not like you're ever going to have a better time, responsibility-free and all."

He went back to eating, like he hadn't just suggested something *insane.*

It was one thing to wonder—one thing to drunkenly talk about a family I never knew, or even one thing to get test results and obsessively Google the people listed on the paper.

That was—not real. It was just, well, a fantasy.

But going to see them? Talking to them? Seeing if I had their laugh, the same long, slightly crooked nose?

"I don't know if that's a good idea," I said.

Griff's eyebrows raised. He shoveled in a bite of hash browns. "Mhhph mmm-mmph."

"Disgusting and unintelligible."

"Why don't you think it's a good idea?"

"Just, like, is it really a good idea? To go and confront these people?" I shook my head. "I could always just connect with them online." I didn't need to travel all the way to— where were they from? Benton? Bennett? Bennett Wood, that was it. It had taken a deep dive into a few distant Instagrams, but I was pretty sure that was where the family was from. *My* family was from. I didn't need to travel all the way to Bennett Wood.

"That's a good point, but—"

I cut him off. "On the other hand, actually *going* there puts me at the advantage. I could scope them out, maybe ask about them, before actually letting them know I was there." It would be the first time in my relationship with my birth family that I was the one who knew something, instead of them.

"That's true, and—"

"And I would be able to leave at any time. I'd also be able to *make* them talk to me, make them *see* me, beyond getting just a read notification and no response online."

"Super good point." Griff nodded. "This conversation, which is one-sided by the way, coming to any conclusion?"

Rolling my eyes, I lifted my coffee. I took a sip as I considered.

What was stopping me? Griff was right; things were perfect for a trip like this. If I got a job, a new apartment lease, I'd never have an opportunity like this again.

"Yes. Yes. I'm gonna do it."

I pretended like the jittering nerves in my hands were from the caffeine and not from the decision I'd just made:

I was going to Bennett Wood and I was going to meet my birth family.

Holy shit.

Chapter 2 - *Jay*

The hot North Carolina sun beamed in through the windows of my truck. The AC was blasting as high as the knob would turn but it didn't care to do much. I was sweating, thick droplets of it sliding down the sides of my face.

I had just finished my last gig, dropping off the cargo at a loading dock just outside of Raleigh. I'd left the trailer and was driving a bobtail now, just driving the tractor. I didn't have another job set up for the next few weeks and while this normally would fill me with relief, happiness at getting off the road for a little bit and stretching my legs, knowledge of where I was headed weighed me down.

Next stop, Bennett Wood. My hometown.

I hadn't been home in a long while, life on the road keeping me busy and far away from the sleepy town I had raced from when I first turned eighteen. But now I was thirty miles out and there was no avoiding it.

There was a crackling sound, like air twisting in on itself, as the radio lit up. I picked it up, answering the call.

Another trucker was on the line, his voice muffled with static. "Bear in the bushes ahead of you, Big Truck."

"Bird dog?" I craned my neck, squinting. I couldn't see the cop's car, but there was a bend in the road that would hide him pretty well. If the other trucker was right, a cop was lying in wait to catch speeders. I eased off the gas.

The radio crackled. "Affirmative." I glanced at the speedometer and slowly pressed on the brake, making sure to graze just at sixty-eight in the seventy, so that the cop's radar gun wouldn't pick me up for speeding.

"10-4," I said, signaling my thanks and hanging up the radio connection. I passed the bend in the road, the cop's car jutting just a little out from a hidden road, and I smirked as I coasted past him.

The life of a truck driver could be lonely—long hours on the road, no stable home, no roots. But there were small perks; the pay, for one, was nothing to turn my nose up at, and the small community, built between radio waves and rest stops, was one that had been welcoming to me at a time when nothing had felt like that. Well, my mom *tried*. She tried her best.

But creating a welcoming community for a gay teenager with no dad and no friends wasn't exactly an easy task for her.

Up next was the exit for Bennett Wood.

I needed to stop thinking about ghosts.

My mom had tried her best and it wasn't fair to expect more from her, especially now that she was gone.

I was on my way home to pack up her belongings, deal with her affairs, and sell her house. Mom had been gone for nearly two years now. There was only so long I could avoid it.

My blinker sounded less like the methodical ticking I was used to and more like a warning. Sweat dripped from my brow and I wiped it away, too hard. I hissed from the pain of my fingernails scraping against my skin.

I hadn't stepped foot in Bennett Wood yet, or, well, tire, and I was already rubbed raw from the mere idea of it.

I should have driven straight to the house, called the lawyer that I was meant to meet, and gotten it all over with as soon as I drove into town. I could get the whole thing dealt with today; hell, if I tried hard enough, I could probably be back on the road by a week from now.

I took the exit and held my breath as the truck rolled into the town's limits.

Everything looked exactly the same.

The faded blue paint on the sign, the dangerous curve into town, the street billing with families holding hands and shops that looked frozen in time.

The sun was bright, directly overhead, and I had to squint to make out the signs and structures as my truck came into town. I didn't need it, though; muscle memory pulled me through the roads, breaking absently as I rolled toward a stop sign. I felt—not dizzy, not lightheaded, but truly not quite present. Not quite there, even as I was acutely aware that I was very much there.

I was only three blocks from my mother's house. Would it be covered in dust? The pictures and knickknacks coated from years of disinterest, the furniture dirty with disuse. What would it feel like, to walk up the slightly crooked sidewalk, my mother's flowerbeds empty? It had been so long since I had been here.

My chest ached.

I pulled into Dilly's Diner, my truck sliding too fast into the parking lot. I drove to the farthest corner of the lot, cutting the engine.

There was certainly no food at my mother's house. Certainly. So, really, heading to her house first was pointless; if I went there, I would need to leave shortly anyway. I had been on the road nearly ten hours today, leaving early at dawn, and should eat first.

It was better to face ghosts on a full stomach, anyway.

The bell above Dilly Diner's front door sent me back two decades. I froze with one hand curled around the handle, chest hammering as I felt myself shrink back into my eighteen-year-old body.

I swallowed hard, squared my shoulders, and ignored the way heads swiveled to me. There was a quiet hush over the diner, interrupted by soft, indistinguishable whisperings that reminded me how quickly gossip moved in Bennett Wood. By nightfall, everyone would know that Jay Richardson was back home.

I sat at the counter, tugging a bit at my hat before sighing and removing it. The waitress popped up, smiling politely. She was young, probably a teenager, and looked at me with curiosity but clear awareness that I was not anyone that she knew or already had an opinion on. It was nice to be unknown, when I knew that likely would not last soon.

I ordered quickly, thanking her, and pulled out my phone.

I took a deep breath and called the realtor.

The waitress dropped off my sweet tea and I took a sip as the line rang. *God,* that was good. Truck driving took me all over but nowhere had sweet sun tea the way Dilly's did.

"Hello?"

I startled, nearly choking, and swallowed. "Uh, hi. This is Jay. Richardson."

"Ah, Mr. Richardson, how're you doing, sir?"

"Good, thank you," I ducked my head, keeping my voice low. "I'm just calling about our meetin'. How would tomorrow work, instead of today? I'm only just arrivin' in town."

"Sure, sure, Mr. Richardson. How's three tomorrow?"

The entry bell rang again and my head snapped up automatically, my eyes drawn instantly to the door.

Standing there, his eyes narrowed as they swept across the diner, was the handsomest man I had ever seen.

The buzzing of the diner seemed to still, as if there was nothing in the room at all but him. His brown hair was cropped short, but the tendrils long enough to curl from sweat just a little at the edge of his hairline. His jaw was sharp, punctuated by a thin layer of hair, a five o'clock shadow coming on a little bit too early. He was wearing a jean jacket and black pants that hugged his long legs—it was much too hot to be dressed like that. His face was flushed, cheeks bright pink, and his lips were parted as if he was breathing deeply.

I couldn't tear my gaze away as he stepped fully into the diner and peeled his jean jacket away. He slung it over his arm, pulling at the thin material of his t-shirt to let air pass.

I had never seen him before—he looked young, but not so young that I wouldn't have had the chance to see him the last time I was in town, surely. My mouth dried as he ran his hand through his hair, the long slope of his body stretching and twisting.

His eyes swept across the diner until they landed on me. They widened, his expression dropping for just a moment, before a slow smile pulled at his lips.

"Mr. Richardson? Sir? Sir!"

I jolted, my face burning as I remembered I was still on the line with the realtor.

I apologized quickly, agreeing to meet her tomorrow, and hung up quickly before I could embarrass myself more.

I set my phone down, ignoring the burn in my cheeks and ears, and grabbed my sweet tea. I took a long drink and the waitress popped by to refill it as soon as I set it down.

"Food's on the way," she said, smiling and quickly darting off to bring my plates over.

The stool next to me squeaked and I glanced over, freezing just for a moment when the handsome stranger sat next to me.

Up close, he was even more startling. His eyes were a light hazel, specks of gold and brown decorating them. Wide, with thick lashes framing them, his eyes were bright with open and unabashed curiosity as he looked at me.

He was tanned, a smooth look that was too golden to be fake, the sort of look you got from hours spent in the sun. His t-shirt clung to him and thick, fat drops of sweat slid down his neck and across his sharp cheekbones. He swiped at it absently, tongue darting out to slip across his bottom lip, and he smiled at me. My breath caught.

"Oh, that looks good." He said, nodding his head toward the counter. I glanced where he was looking, surprised that my food had materialized without me noticing.

I cleared my throat. "Oh, erm, yeah."

The food did look good. My mouth was too dry to even consider eating it.

He cocked his head, the tip of his tongue sticking out as his eyes flickered across me. His smile widened and he turned away.

I grabbed my sweet tea and downed half of it in one go.

The waitress came back over with a pitcher, topping off my glass, and took the man's order.

He hummed briefly and said, "I'll take what he had."

The waitress poured him a glass of sweet tea before darting off.

He took a drink of his tea, glancing around the room. I watched him from the corner of my eye, the way he slowly considered every inch of the diner. His eyes lingered on the customers but darted away before anyone noticed.

His eyes fell back to me. He dropped one elbow to the counter, one palm cradling his chin, fingers resting on his cheek. "I'm Joshua."

I swallowed around a sudden lump, taking a careful moment to squeeze the eagerness out of my voice. "Jay."

Slowly, he leaned in a little, just a small twist of his body that seemed nearly unconscious as he shifted closer to me. "Nice to meet you."

I couldn't help the small smile that tugged at me.

Maybe this trip to Bennett Wood wouldn't be all bad, after all.

Chapter 3 - *Joshua*

The man sitting next to me at the counter of this small North Carolina diner was blushing.

It was hot as hell outside and I knew that he was probably flushed from the heat anyway, but there was a distinctively darker shade of a red on his cheeks now that I had introduced myself.

I couldn't remember the last time my mere presence had made a guy blush—surely it wasn't a regular occurrence back at the dorm parties I'd been to. And this guy was clearly older—a decade? Even two?—from anyone else I'd been interested in. I wasn't used to finding older men attractive, or trying to flirt with them. Hell, I wasn't used to flirting in general.

It wasn't that I had never been with a guy, it was just that I was—unpracticed. The majority of my experiences were drunken scrambles that had little to do with active decision-making. It was equally my awkward attempts at romance and my hang-ups from too many conservative foster parents that led to me being a fumbling mess when I tried to flirt with anyone.

But this guy, with his strong jaw and blushing cheeks—he was maybe worth the attempt.

He smelled *good* and his smile, though small, was sort of incredible. Pine wood and heat, sort of like a Christmas bonfire, even though it was nowhere near the holiday season. It was like jittery excitement, being out late when you weren't used to it, laughing from your friends, safe from your family— it was a poignant scent. His lips were big, plush red pillows that he kept wetting with the tip of his tongue. It was distracting and I felt nearly voyeuristic, unable to stop my eyes from dropping down to them.

The waitress dropped my food off. My stomach growled and this seemed to remind the stranger that his food was growing cold in front of him.

"That looks good," I said, nodding at our matching plates.

Jay's eyes flickered to the plates and then back to me. "Yeah, it does."

We ate in relative silence, the low buzz of the diner a white noise machine to our scraping forks and chewing. I could feel the way my body was fidgeting, adjusting on the stool as I tried to eat in the least gross way possible.

I had been driving for over seven hours, snacking on the jerky and chips I had packed with me for the trip, but as soon as I smelled the plate of fried chicken, I had realized just how hungry I was.

The food was good—the crispiness of the chicken and the smooth coleslaw a delicious meal regardless of how ravenous I felt.

Jay ate his food with equal enthusiasm. While he ate, focused on his food in a quiet, easy way that made me think he must've eaten a lot of meals alone, I looked at him from the corner of my eye.

He had broad shoulders, thick with clear muscles evident even beneath the thin flannel he was wearing. They turned in slightly, his spine curving, as he hunched over his plate. He wore faded blue jeans, nearly white around the knees, and boots that looked too hot to have on during this sweltering weather. On the counter next to his drink was a dark green baseball cap, the bill bent a little like it was old and well-worn. The flannel he was wearing had the sleeves pushed to his elbows and along with two simple silver bands, he wore an elaborate ring that looked like a family crest.

Altogether, it made for an interesting image—even hunched over on a stool and fully clothed, I could tell the man had a nice frame, a good body; the kind of body professional athletes had, strong from the inside out. He dressed like a farmer but had the jewelry of a reclusive aristocrat.

It was weird. He was probably weird.

I was more than a little into it.

He caught me staring and I looked away quickly, shoving a spoonful of baked beans in my mouth before I could say something stupid.

I had been in Bennett Wood for twenty minutes. I shouldn't be ogling the locals. I was here for a *mission*—as of right now, a secret mission. What was I doing?

Not only was this not a good idea, I would probably be bad at it! I didn't flirt. I didn't even know how.

But, then again—wasn't the point of this trip to push my limits? Maybe this wasn't what my friends had in mind when they encouraged me to leave, but, hell, I had a hard time thinking that any one of them *wouldn't* want me to try to hook up with the hot weird diner guy.

I took a deep breath, a long gulp of sweet tea—god, that was sugary—and then twisted on my stool.

"You from around here?" I winced a little, worried that my voice was lecherous as the line slid out accidentally.

Jay's hands froze, knife and fork hesitating over his plate, and he turned, just a little.

His eyes found mine, and just as quickly as he had frozen, he relaxed. He cleared his throat, the sound sharp, and then lifted and dropped one shoulder.

I frowned. "You're not sure?"

The corner of his mouth lifted. "Not quite."

Huh.

"Me either."

It was an odd thing to have in common—this inability to place exactly what Bennett Wood meant to us. For me, it was the potential that this was the place that my roots started; the place where my family was, where I began.

The nerves that felt like electric sugar in my veins, too strong to let me rest or breathe or do anything but *shake* nervously, were back. I had been drowning in nerves for days now.

For just a minute, I needed to steady myself—remind myself that I existed outside of this hunt, this pursuit of people that hadn't wanted me, didn't know me. Bennett Wood was full of potential, and I had no idea which way my luck would fall.

I swallowed past the nerves and focused again on my surprise dining partner.

I didn't imagine that Jay was also here to find his birth family. I didn't want to pry, so I went back to my food, waiting to see if he'd divulge anything more. I didn't really want to be alone with my thoughts, but the man was quiet and I didn't want to bug him. Even if he *had* seemed interested, it was brief, and I knew better than to assume that older, gruff-looking men were cool with me having an interest in them. It was always better—safer—to let them lead the way.

I did my best to ignore him in a polite way. The hum of chatter and scraping utensils filled the space. After a minute, where he alternated between staring at me with squinted eyes and focusing on his food, he sighed. "I'm from here, but I'm just—drifting through."

A flash of excitement went through me. "Missed the sweet tea?"

His lips quirked. "Among other things."

He was tight-lipped.

I quite liked his lips. I glanced away and hid my smile behind another sip.

"My mom's place has been empty for a while now. I'm here to sell it. No use leaving it empty to rot." He answered after a beat. Then, in the same breath. "Why are you in town?"

I tilted my head, considering. If Jay was from here, there was a chance, however small, that he actually *knew* the people I was here for. I didn't want to risk them finding out about me before I found them—the chance of bolting quickly, without any interactions, was still deeply appealing to me.

I shrugged, mimicking his own indifference. "Just drifting through, sort of."

He watched me with rapt attention and I couldn't stop myself from barreling forward. "I just graduated college. I didn't have anything lined up and, well, I don't know. Now just seemed as good a time as any to hit the road."

"Have you been driving long?"

"Nah, just today. This is my first non-gas stop, actually. Have you taken a road trip before?"

Jay nodded. "In a way."

I waited for him to elaborate. When he didn't, I couldn't stop the burst of laughter. "Are you *trying* to be mysterious?"

His eyes widened and a small smile twitched on his lips. "No."

Jay didn't elaborate. I laughed again and he seemed to notice his mistake. "I'm a truck driver. I do a lot of long-haul and so I've spent a good amount of time on the road."

"But you've never taken an actual road trip?" I surmised.

He shook his head. I noticed that in the dimming light, as the sun started to set outside of the wide diner windows, Jay's hair was a little lighter than I originally thought; streaks of bronze and blond in the slight waves. I was caught by the way the curls were just a little long, tucked behind his ears.

"Not really," he said with another shrug. He had set his fork down, twisted in his stool now so that he was facing me completely. I set my utensils down, pushing my half-full plate away, and propped my elbow on the table, dropping my chin to my curled palm.

"You should try it sometime," I said, watching as he mimicked my position, his body mirroring mine.

"You're enjoying your trip so far?" He quirked an eyebrow.

I swallowed around my suddenly dry mouth. "It's had its—good points."

"That so?" There was a look in his eye I hadn't noticed before. Interest. *Jackpot.*

"Yes," I could hear the slight tease in his voice now.

The tip of Jay's tongue peeked out from between his lips, wetting the swell of his bottom lip. There was a moment, brief as it was heavy, where Jay looked at me with such clear interest and contemplation that I couldn't force myself to move at all—even my breath lay trapped in my lungs, unable to adjust even slightly.

With a start, I realized that I wanted to close the space between us, wanted to hear what sound he'd make if I kissed him here and now—surprised or sure? Would he kiss me back?

I nearly shook at the urge.

Still, I held myself back.

I didn't know what I was doing, not really. I had barely been in town an hour and, yeah, the guy was hot and interested and nice, but this wasn't me.

I wanted to know what he felt like pressed against me—it felt like the prickling of a headache, unavoidable and poignant.

I couldn't make my body move or words to come out of my mouth, though. I had no idea what to do now.

I waited and hoped that Jay would make the next step.

The waitress came over and dropped off our checks. I barely managed a cursory thank you, still drawn by the way Jay's eyes were flickering across me.

They fell to my lips, narrowed, and then a smooth smile came across his face.

The hesitancy that Jay had been hiding behind earlier seemed to momentarily disappear, something surer and stronger peeking out from behind his expression, and I shivered.

He pulled out his wallet and glanced at the check. I reached for mine, my hand shaking just slightly.

He held out a hand and I froze. "I'll get it."

"Oh, you don't—"

He stopped me with a wry smile and quirked eyebrow. "It's the least I can do for you keepin' me company."

I swallowed. *Say something. He's about to leave.* "Thank you," I squeaked out instead.

A flash across his face, tongue peeking out again, and then he shrugged it off. "You're welcome."

He dropped two twenties on the counter and stood, his back arching just slightly as he stretched. He grabbed his jacket, slugged it over one arm, and then put his hat back on. It cast a shadow on his face.

I had to crane my neck up to look at him, his body thick and towering over me as I sat on my stool, dumbfounded. *He's leaving! Do something.* I was frozen.

"Course," he said slowly, eyes dragging across the diner before stopping again on me. "Company doesn't have to end."

I swallowed hard. "No?"

"I'm headed back to my mom's place—it's been empty for a while, so there might be some dust, but. Hell. If you wanted to—*keep* keepin' me company, you're welcome to join."

My heart skipped a beat. I tilted my head, just a little. His lips twitched.

Gotcha.

A slow smile pulled at my lips. "Uh. Yeah. Yes."

He grinned and held out a hand. After a small pause, I slid my hand into his and let him help me off the stool. Though he dropped my hand as soon as I was standing, my fingers and palm burned from the contact well after we went into the parking lot and he instructed me to follow his truck.

This was certainly not what I was expecting out of my day.

But, hell. I could roll with the punches if they were like *this.* My stomach fluttered and I decided I didn't mind this distraction at all.

Chapter 4 - *Jay*

There was heat pouring through my skin that had nothing to do with the Carolina sun.

Joshua's little blue car had followed me down the winding roads and the five-minute drive had felt like *hours*. But now, we were parked by the edge of the street and my mother's house didn't look half as boarded or scary as I had imagined it would.

It was hard to focus on the dead flowerbeds and grimy windows when Joshua's body was emanating heat right next to me. He was bouncing on the balls of his feet while I unlocked the front door.

It creaked open, and I was grateful that I had called ahead last week and hired a cleaner to come in and do a quick sweep of the place. It still was distinctly unlived in, but there was a sheen of Pine Sol and bleach in the house that made it at least feel clean.

Joshua looked around, stepping out of his shoes as he closed the door behind him.

I didn't bother watching him take in the house for the first time; I was struggling taking it all in myself.

Muscle memory had me out of my boots and walking toward the living room without a second thought. The AC was a window unit and took a good minute to start up, but the second that the cold air burst through, I felt a tension in my shoulders relax.

What was I doing? Bringing a stranger back here—he was a kid, basically, in his early twenties which was a lifetime ago for me. But he was handsome and smart and interested and, hell, where was the harm in finding a little solace? I had done this dozens of times—picking someone up on the road, bringing them back to my room and having a little fun, for both of us, guaranteed. It never turned into anything more, but it was okay like that—easy.

Being in this town, it didn't feel easy. I could feel myself trying to shrink back into a life I had barely lived decades ago.

The ache of wanting to settle down, something that had been scratching at the back of my head for months now, the ache of wanting something more, something that had any meaning—that ache was still there, asking me if this was really a good idea.

With our age difference, not to mention that we were both just passing through, there wasn't a shot in hell that this would be anything more than a little fun.

But, hell.

Maybe a little fun wasn't a bad idea. I just—had to have reasonable expectations, was all. This wouldn't become anything.

Two hands closed around my shoulders and I jumped.

Joshua's hands froze and then, a beat, and he started to gently massage. His hands were a little too light, not quite as rough as I liked, but the feeling still had the tension leaking out of my body and I suddenly forgot what I was worried about.

I turned, slowly, shivering as the AC hit the back of my neck.

Joshua was a tall man, but fell just a few inches shorter than my six-five frame. Now that he was here, I could look at him fully, without worrying about being rude or drawing unwanted attention from the other patrons at the diner.

Joshua's golden brown eyes flickered across my face, drinking me in the same way I was drinking him in.

He was *pretty*, his lips a soft red and his skin a smooth tan; he was smiling, just a little, his cheeks round with the effort to keep his smile small.

I swallowed hard, my hands trembling at my side with excitement.

This was not what I thought I'd be doing with my evening—

Joshua leaned in, his hands flying to my waist, tugging me to close the space between us, and his eyes fell to my lips and his grin grew. His fingers slid in my belt loops, and he tilted his head, mouth teasing just a few inches away from me.

—I was *not* upset by the turn of events.

I closed the space between us and as our lips pressed against each other, my pulse nearly stopped, my heart clenching and freezing in my chest. For just one moment, everything was quiet, still—a breath away from cracking, glass too cold and about to shatter against the heat of hands.

His mouth was sweet. He tasted like sun tea and mint.

Joshua was warm, pliable against me, his body molding against mine. His arms wound around me, the tips of his fingers toying with the hair at the nape of my neck. Fingernails scratched the sensitive skin there. The window unit blew onto my back, shivers from either side of my body forcing a powerful tremble to blow through me.

We broke away, both gasping for air. Joshua wasted no time and attached his mouth to my neck, lips and tongue soothing over the nips of his teeth as he worked dutifully.

"Joshua," his name came out hoarse, my voice strained even in its quiet whisper.

He hummed, punctuating the vibrations of his lips against my throat with a light kiss. He let his fingers find a good grip in my hair and then tugged *hard,* my head snapping back, giving him more room to work.

A low curse burst out of my chest, sparks flying from his rough tug all the way to my fingertips, and suddenly I wasn't frozen at all anymore.

I pulled away, ignoring his affronted expression, and grabbed his hand, tugging him toward the couch. I sat down and Joshua grinned, looking much less boyish now that a hungry shadow was covering his face, and he scrambled to sit on my lip.

He ran his fingers through my hair, the subtle scraping hypnotic in its absolute deliciousness. I grab his chin, holding him firmly in my grasp as I drank in his wide eyed expression.

He straddled my lap, holding himself just off of me, his hands curled around the top of the couch to steady himself. He panted, just a little, his pulse racing in his neck—I could see the way he was struggling to stay still, desperate to squirm and relieve the building tension he must have been feeling.

His eyes were just a thin gold sliver around pure black pupil, his high cheeks adorned with a soft pink flush. His lips were bitten red and spit-shiny and I was dizzy with the punching lust in my gut.

He was devastatingly *beautiful.*

I yanked his chin gently toward me, and swallowed his surprised gasp.

Lips and tongues fought against each other for dominance. Joshua wasn't trying to hold back, the scrape of his teeth and slick push of his tongue against me absolutely, debilitatingly filthy.

The push of his body against mine had me gasping for air sooner than I would have liked and I tore away, groaning loudly as he attached his lips to my neck. Licking and sucking softly against the sensitive skin there, my hips were shifting, tilting up toward the friction of his hips.

He sank down on me, hard through his too tight jeans, and I hissed out an appreciative groan.

"Fuck," the curse tumbled out from my lips, and he dove against my mouth to swallow it.

He leaned back a little and my arms wound around him to hold him heavy on my lap.

"Jay," he said, voice muffled from the way he was curled, face pressed in my neck. I ran one of my hands up his back, underneath his t-shirt, feeling myself grow heavy as he slowly ground against me.

"Can we—do you—" he was struggling to ask what he wanted, but his little whiny mewls were easy to interpret.

"Get up," I ordered, wincing at how gruff I sounded. Joshua scrambled off my lap, though, eyes wide, still panting, and I filed that away for later consideration.

I smirked at him, closing the space between us and winding my fingers in his short hair, tugging him closer and giving him a searing kiss. He nearly fell into me, arms around my neck, and I bit down hard enough on his bottom lip for him to moan loudly in my mouth before I pulled away again, gently kissing on the swell.

While he was still staring at me in a daze, chest heaving, I made quick work of pulling the sofa bed out, quickly tossing the cushions out the way. It was a bit of a buzzkill to worry about now but Joshua caught on quickly and helped me.

As soon as it was ready, I grabbed him by the thin t-shirt he wore and tugged him down, watching him bounce pleasantly against the mattress.

We undressed quickly, not bothering to make a show of it, and when we were both only in boxers, I joined him on the bed, covering his body with mine.

"Oh, *fuck!*" he exclaimed when I slid against him slowly, the swells of our hot cocks sliding against each other.

I mouthed at his neck, relishing in the small sounds Joshua couldn't help but blurt out, holding myself up with one arm while the other snaked between us. Joshua's hands were above his head, fisted tightly in the material of the pillow, and I watched with a wide grin as his face scrunched up, knuckles going white, when my fingertips slid beneath his boxers and grazed the weeping tip of his cock.

My eyes squeezed shut as I fought against a tremble building in my spine. His tip was leaking precum, velvety smooth against my coarse fingertips. His body twisted and writhed beneath me, his chest heaving, and I couldn't stop myself from wrapping my hand fully around him.

My own jumping, aching cock was forgotten as I watched Joshua's face, his eyes popping open wide and his mouth falling. I kept my fist tight, slowly moving up and down, letting the dry burn fade into a wet glide as more and more gathered at the tip, collecting against my thumb as I raked it across him.

He was blathering now, words or pleas or groans blending together into nothing. It was *music*.

I could tell when he was reaching his breaking point, his whole body tensing and his hips fighting to quicken my pace, and then I pulled off.

I nearly laughed at the devastation on his face, his whole body spasming before relaxing, his cock jumping as it searched for friction.

His eyes were wild and unfocused as he looked at me, before narrowing dangerously into slits.

I leaned down, pressing a firm kiss on his lips before he could protest. Then, slowly, I reached down and slid his boxers fully down his legs, pressing small kisses against his chin, his neck, his collarbone as he helped me fully undress him. I kicked my own boxers off unceremoniously, leaning back on my thighs to drink him in.

Joshua was sprawled across the bed, cheeks bright red, chest lifting and falling rapidly. He had pushed himself up on his elbows and the blush he wore dipped down his smooth chest, gathering at his abs. His hard, long cock was a *sight,* standing straight, a plum red, slick with his own precum that I had spread along the length. Light blond curls rested at the base of it and I could barely stop myself from swallowing him down.

"You're a tease," he said, breathless.

I knew I was grinning wolfishly. "You've been a good boy."

His cock jumped again. "Yeah?" It was practically a wheeze.

"Yeah," I repeated, leaning over him. I hovered, just a little out of reach, and a small growl vibrated from Joshua's chest as he reached up, fisting my hair, and crashing our lips together.

It was wet and desperate and so good that we were back to grinding against each other in wild abandon.

My own tension was growing hot in my belly and I forcefully pulled away. "Shit."

"Condoms?" he asked.

I practically leapt from the bed, going over to my bag, and digging around. I pulled out a small bottle of lube and shrugged, tossing it to him. He caught it easily and I went back to searching.

It took long enough that I was starting to catch my breath, pulse evening out, before I found them in a side pocket.

When I turned back to the bed, triumphant in my condom retrieval, all the heat that had dissipated came rushing back fast enough to give me a headrush. I was dizzy and on fire, my jaw dropping as I stared at the unbelievable sight in front of me.

One arm long against the bed, his feet splayed flat, Joshua was holding himself up. His neck was long, head lolling back and his eyes closed. His long cock was bobbing up and down against his stomach, and he had one arm twisted behind his body, three fingers working fast and hard inside of him.

"Fuck," it was punched out from me along with my breath, watching as Joshua quickly worked himself. The lube was open, spilling a little on the bedspread, and I could see it dripping down his knuckles and wrist.

"Fuck," I repeated, before quickly rejoining him.

"Took you long enough," his words were haughty but it was undercut by the trembling lips and gasping tone.

I couldn't take it any longer. I grabbed him, barely stopping myself from fully manhandling him, and laid him against the bed. He grinned wide, eyes blown.

I slid the condom onto me, grabbing the bottle of lube to slick myself up, and bent down for another quick kiss. Sliding one hand underneath his knee, his other leg spreading, foot dropping to the floor as his thighs parted, and I slid into him in one slow push.

"Aghhh, *fuck*!" he yelled out, his hands flying to my back, nails digging in hard.

I could feel the pinch of his nails against my skin, feel the way his ass was fluttering around my cock, and I ground my teeth together to stop myself from hammering into him.

When his eyes cleared a little, the heels of his hands pushed into my back, encouraging me to move. Slowly, I pulled my hips back and pushed into him again, groaning loud at the tight heat swelling around me.

"Fuck yeah, please," he let out, head falling back. His jaw was sharp and his Adam's apple bobbed. I bent down, hips still slow as I fucked into him, the slow, desperate heat nearly driving me crazy, and bit down on his jaw, swiping my tongue against the mark.

His cock was trapped between us, hot and wet, and Joshua licked his way into my mouth. "Please, please, please, fuck, oh." He didn't stop his pleas, hooking his leg around my waist, and using his whole body to fuck up against me.

My whole body was shaking, sweat dripping down my chest, and Joshua pulled away, a desperate whine in his throat. "Jay, please, please. Fuck me."

Well.

I didn't need to be asked twice.

My hips snapped hard, and his answering moan reverberated off the walls. I fucked him hard, in earnest, our hips sliding against each other. Each new thrust of my hips buried my cock deeper and deeper in him, his wanton moans and breathy pants in my ears.

I held onto his hips tight, fingers digging in, and he had one hand still on my back, the other tightly fisting my hair as he pulled himself up and met me with each hard thrust.

Sweat was building between us, dripping down my chest and between my shoulder blades. It dripped from his hairline, where the small curls were pressed to his forehead, down onto his swollen red lips.

He was writhing, nails digging in, and his cock was throbbing from where it was trapped between us. Feeling him squirm the way he was had me near the brink sooner than I would have liked, and I was desperate to get him off first, but couldn't get a hand to him.

He was cursing quietly under his breath, a soft litany of pleas between clenched teeth.

I sank lower, feeling the hot, tight heat of my balls press against his sweaty skin, bit down on his collarbone, fucked hard and fast as his cock twitched and throbbed between us.

"Oh, oh, Jay, please, *oh, shit,*" his voice dipped low, and he crooned out more pleas.

"Yeah, yeah," I fucked him harder, right where I was as he continued to chant *yes* over and over again. He was nearly locked into place, limbs around me, his whole body tight and trembling. He was so close and I was nearly there, too. "Yeah, yeah, sweetheart, come for me."

His eyes shot open, wide, and his body stilled. "Jay," he cried out, my name sounding like melting cotton candy on his tongue, and then he was spilling between us, his whole body quivering and tight and—

I slammed my hips as far as I could, my own body locking up as it pushed through me.

My vision blacked out and when I came to, I was lying next to Joshua, both of us panting heavily.

Taking off the condom, I groaned, and when my legs stopped shaking, I went and threw it away. I brought back a wet towel. Joshua took it from me, his hands shaking, and he cleaned himself off.

"Uh," he cleared his throat. "I, um, wow."

I grinned, already lying back down. My heart was still hammering in my chest.

"I guess I should head out—"

"Stay," I said, throwing one arm over my head. I couldn't remember ever feeling this tired or relaxed. Every bit of my body felt like Jell-O. "It's late, just stay the night."

I could hear him shifting, the cranking of the air conditioning, crickets outside—

I fell asleep before Joshua replied.

Chapter 5 - *Joshua*

I woke up with a start, my heart racing.

Creaking one eye open, I frowned at the unfamiliar space—there was an old TV, the boxed kind that I only had vague memories of using as a kid in a basement. The walls were so floral that it was nearly blinding.

I tried to roll over, groaning, but was stopped by a hard, thick wall. I forced both eyes open and came face to face with a firm, tanned chest.

Oh, fuck.

My pulse was still racing as I came to my senses, memories of last night flooding me. Jay was still asleep, his face relaxed, one arm thrown carelessly over me. There was a slight vibration emanating from his chest; I could feel it against my body, we were so tightly pressed together.

My body was a little sore. I winced as I slowly stretched out, feeling my legs tremble a little.

Last night was—

Very, very good.

The anxious awakening I'd had worked better than a cup of coffee; I was wide awake, trying to keep myself from moving too much and waking Jay up, too.

I wasn't a one-night stand kind of guy—that was, I wasn't *against* a casual hookup. Clearly. It was just more that my experience was drunken fumblings at a party, not sleep-over-and-cuddle-in-the-morning.

I should leave.

It wasn't rude—Jay had been generous, offering me a place to stay because I was tired and spent and it was late. But he hadn't, like, asked me out.

I slowly and carefully slid out from underneath his arms, sliding out of the covers. My bare feet padded across the living room floor, the air conditioner blowing on my bare ass and I shivered as I gathered my clothes.

I slipped into the bathroom, wrinkling my nose at the state of myself. I did a quick wash, scrubbing at my face with the hand soap, and swished some mouthwash. I dressed quickly and, shoes in my hand, I slid out of the front door as quietly as I could.

Jay rolled over when I was halfway through closing the door and I froze. He grumbled before relaxing again.

I breathed out a sigh of relief and tiptoed to my car.

I was glad that I had parked across the street and there was no way that the rumbling of my car would wake Jay up. It wasn't that I didn't want to see him again, necessarily—it was just—awkward.

I was awkward.

It was a good night, a nice distraction, but I should get back to what I was actually in Bennett Wood to do.

I drove around town, looking for a place to stay, and decided to skip on the nicer motel I saw in favor of a campsite a few miles outside of town. It was significantly cheaper and, considering the budget I had, which was all of my savings, and my lack of job prospects, cheaper was better.

I took a quick shower once I'd checked in and dressed in clean clothes, before climbing back in my car and pulling out the folder I'd packed that had the info from my DNA matches.

The site that my friends had used to get my results was pretty standard, as far as I could tell. With a bit of my spit, it had given me a full rundown of my ethnicity—a whole bunch of random bits and pieces that essentially said, *you're a white dude*—and any matches in the system. As it was, not everyone was there, of course, but it connected me to the distant relations I might have had, and the ones that my relatives might've had.

There were nearly a dozen matches found, but two in particular were closest: both physically from my old Kentucky apartment and genetically.

I glanced down at the print-off sheet that read *Luke Selwyn.* This guy was supposed to be my half-brother.

And holy shit, if that hadn't sent me to bed for a week as I tried to wrap my head around the idea that I, Joshua Matthews, had a goddamn brother after all.

I'd found Luke's social media last week, a careful search on Instagram and Facebook, but I hadn't reached out. It—was too much. What if Luke didn't care? What if he had known about me all along and just didn't want to know me? What if—

I put away that sheet, ignoring how my hands shook, and glanced at the other person who I knew was in Bennett Wood.

Bernice Selwyn.

It didn't say who she was to me, but based off of her age and last name, I thought maybe a great-aunt or something. She was what brought me to Bennett Wood.

It wasn't that I would be okay with Bernice rejecting me, the way that Luke or any of the others might. It was just—well, I thought it would sting a little less. Some random old lady might be less—*impactful*—as a brother might be.

I hoped I was right about that, at least.

And, too, if I knew anything about little old ladies in small towns, it was that they had the scoop. My friends and I had decided that if anyone knew what was going on with the biological family I didn't know, this woman would be a good bet.

It had taken a bit of Googling, but I had found an address from Bernice on the south side of town. Double-checking it with the map I had pulled up on my phone, I took a deep breath and packed away the folder, tossing it into the back of the car, and started my drive.

I grabbed a coffee and donut from a drive-thru, trying to keep track of the price for when I freaked out at my bank account later. Jay buying my dinner last night was a surprise, but a good one. I wasn't so pinched I couldn't afford it, but hell, a little free meal never hurt.

I drove through the sleepy town, watching as it woke up. There were a few people on the streets, women carrying tote bags with bread sticking out, couples walking their dogs, a few dads pushing strollers, but there was an ease in the way they moved, waved to each other. A woman stood outside a store sweeping. It was like a movie. It was only just past seven. I hadn't realized how early I had woken up at Jay's, but it was nice to get a look at Bennett Wood without anyone looking back.

It wasn't a small town really, but more mid-sized. It had a quaint look to it that had me forgetting that it was nearly as big as the town I'd grown up in.

When I pulled up in front of the address, I double-checked on my phone that it was the right place.

A little blue house with broken shutters and a faded white picket fence—the kind of place that ten years ago would've been picturesque.

Two young kids were playing in the front yard, action figures splayed across the grass. A woman was sitting on the stoop, one hand curled around a coffee mug and the other holding a cigarette.

She looked too young to be Bernice—Bernice was supposed to be in her sixties and this woman could've passed for early forties, easily.

I took a deep breath, popped in a breath mint, and then climbed out of the car. The woman's head snapped up and though she didn't move, she did narrow her eyes at me.

"Uh, hi." I lifted one hand to wave, but at her quirked eyebrow, I let it fall awkwardly to my side. I ran my palms down the thighs of my jeans, trying not to squirm. The kids paid me no attention.

The woman gave me a half smile, bordering on a grimace, just a light acknowledging of my presence. "Can I help you?"

"Yeah, uh," I could hear my voice shaking, just a little, my whole body trembling from the adrenaline coursing through me. *Here it goes.* "I'm, uh, looking for— is Bernice Selwyn here?"

The woman's posture relaxed a little, and she shook her head. "Sorry, kid. Nope."

"Oh," disappointment flared, harsh. "Do you know when she'll be back?"

"Uh, never?" She laughed at her own joke.

I frowned. "What do you mean—" I cut myself off, eyes widening. "Is she?"

"Dead?" The woman snorted. "That old bat won't ever bite it."

I felt my hands curl around the wooden fence almost painfully. I hadn't even realized I had drifted close enough to touch it.

The woman sighed and took a drink of her coffee. "She doesn't live here anymore. I bought this place from her estate, like, a few years ago."

"Where is she?" I was surprised at the desperation in my voice.

The woman shrugged. "I don't know. I don't really know her."

I swallowed hard, nodding. I couldn't help the way I shrunk into myself, feeling the crestfallen expression take over my face. The woman must have taken pity on me as I turned away.

"Listen, I do know that she spent a lot of time at that coffee shop off Broadway. Maybe someone there will know where she's at."

A flare of hope pulsed through me. "Thank you!"

She waved me off, but with a small smile on her face. I waved goodbye and half-jogged across the street to my car.

I found the coffee shop pretty quickly. It was busy, people spilling out from it and into the street constantly. It took about three times to parallel park in front of the empty space and a young couple watched me with clear amusement, even as they quickly darted their eyes when I climbed out. I ignored them, my head held high, even knowing I had just completely botched a parking technique we all learned at fifteen.

With the residue of embarrassment sticking to me and the sun starting to peek out hotly from behind the billowy clouds, I darted into the bakery.

I waited in line, foot tapping nervously. A few patrons shot me dirty looks for my apparent impatience and I smiled apologetically. I was so *close* to answers and if these people could just order drips instead of fancy mochas, I could be that much closer.

Eventually, I made my way up the line. The barista knew who I was talking about but not where I could find Bernice. She pointed out the manager and I asked him. He directed me to a church two blocks over.

Following that clue, I quickly walked the short distance, unwilling to try to get out of that tight spot so soon, and took the steps up to the chapel two at a time.

A preacher was at the pulpit and when he noticed me, I quickly relayed my search—albeit a shortened, not-biological-family-searching version.

Thankfully, after a full morning of wild goose chasing, the preacher knew exactly who Bernice was and where to find her.

Which was how I found myself struggling out of my tiny parking spot and heading towards Woods Retirement Home.

The preacher was sure that Bernice was there and that he'd call ahead to warn the receptionist that I was coming.

My hands shook and I curled them tight enough to hurt around the steering wheel.

No matter what she said or what happened, I was about to meet the first blood relative I ever had. My biological family, and the answers I didn't even know how to form questions for, were just a few miles outside of my reach. I swallowed around a sudden lump in my throat.

Here goes nothing.

Chapter 6 - *Jay*

The next morning, I woke up slow and groggy.

The lumpy pull-out bed was too soft and thin for my back; even though I was used to stealing hours in the cab of my truck or budget motels, somehow my mother's terrible couch bed was still the worst thing I had ever slept on.

I groaned, stretching slowly as my muscles protested and body fought with curling in on itself. I rolled onto my back, sighing.

I lazily searched across the room, a little surprised to see that Joshua's presence was swept from the room. He must have snuck out while I was still sleeping. I hoped he at least spent the night; it really was dumb to waste money on a hotel room for half the night.

I had hoped that Joshua would have stayed a little later. Maybe for another early morning round, and some breakfast—anything, really, to prolong our encounter just a bit more.

And, a small, selfish part of me noted, to avoid why I was actually here just a little bit longer.

Oh, well.

I pushed the disappointment aside—a fling was just that. I shouldn't get upset because it ended up being exactly what I knew it was.

I got out of bed, digging in the small duffel I had thrown down last night, and stepped into some boxers, throwing on a t-shirt. Once I was sure the neighbors wouldn't be scarred if the curtains weren't closed, I stumbled toward the kitchen to start the coffee. I was glad that I had remembered to pick up a few things during my last route. The coffee pot had a thin sheen of dust on it and I groaned loudly, annoyed, and wiped at it with the sleeve of my shirt. I ran the water through once to clean it out and then sighed in relief when it bubbled on. If the machine was broken, I'd have to go into town for my cup of Joe and there was little I wanted more than to avoid that.

I did not care for mornings. And mornings that had started off with a backache and a bout of disappointment were *really* not my thing.

I stood a bit mindlessly in the kitchen, listening to the soft gurgling of the pot and trying to wake myself up.

Now that I was standing, my muscles weren't quite as *in pain* as they were nicely sore. Memories of why they were sore helped to lift my mood. The way that Joshua had felt, his fingernails against my skin, his breath hot against my throat, was enough to make any man okay with a bit of soreness and an early morning.

He had said he was just passing through; absently, I wondered if I would see him again before he left. It seemed unlikely but a small part of me was still hopeful.

Once the coffee was finished, I poured myself a mug, and sighed. Looking around, the kitchen seemed as good a place as any to start.

I had to start clearing out the place. The realtor would be by later to take a look and the fewer things that were cluttering up the place, the better. It wasn't necessarily bad, just still had a lot of Mom's things.

I opened the cabinets, taking stock of what was here, while I drank my first mug. Then I went back to my duffel, grabbed out my toiletries, and took a quick shower. I scrubbed my face and brushed my teeth after I got out and dressed quickly. My jeans were a little faded and rubbed raw around the knees and the white t-shirt was tighter than I liked, especially considering how hot it was, which made the flannel I normally wore more of a hazard. Already, the heat was seeping in through the windows. The living room AC unit did little to combat the sun.

Once dressed, I slid on my socks and boots, then refilled my coffee mug.

A decade ago, there had been empty brown boxes in the garage. I took a deep breath, then went out to check.

They were exactly where I remembered them.

I was in a time capsule of my youth and my mother's past. The walls felt too close to me.

My mom's car, an old, clunky, rusting Buick, was parked in the center of the garage. I didn't even realize she still had it. Though, of course, it was still here—I didn't know how I forgot about it. I hoped this was the last forgotten thing I remembered on this trip.

I ignored the sinking feeling and grabbed an armful of boxes, snagging the boxing tape that was collecting dust on a shelf, and kicked the door shut behind me.

"Fuck it," I grumbled, tossing it all on the kitchen floor.

I worked my way through the dishes and random appliances, packing everything but a mug and the coffee pot. It took the majority of morning and by the time the kitchen was all packed up, counters wiped and cabinets cleared out, I had gone through a pot and a half of coffee and had started sweating in earnest. My t-shirt stuck to me and I decided to take a break.

My stomach was starting to gurgle a little uncomfortably. A glance at the clock told me it was nearing noon.

I emptied my mug, rinsing it quickly, and filled it with water. I downed the first cup, gasping a little as I forced myself to slow down, and then refilled it. I moved into the living room and stood in front of the AC, peeling my shirt away from my body to let the air cool me.

I twisted my torso, wincing as my back cracked, and then carefully rolled my neck until that popped, too.

I drank this mug of water slower, letting the water and AC cool me down. With the entire kitchen packed, I needed to get the boxes out of the way.

I went to my bag, digging around a bit until I found my cell phone. It was on its last legs and I cursed, going to charge it. Leaning on the kitchen counter, I plugged it in and then pulled up an internet app.

"Goddamn nothing town," I grumbled, a half-forgotten phrase from my teenage years, when no charity thrift stores came up. There used to be a thrift store in town, but it looked like that closed down a few years ago. There was a retirement home, though. I searched for it, loading the FAQ page to see if they accepted donations.

I finished my water, tapping the bottom of the mug lightly to chase the last few drops, and quickly washed it, leaving it on the counter for later.

Sighing, I glanced back at my truck—it was big, even without the trailer attached, and would be hard to maneuver through town. I frowned and, slow enough it would have been comical to an outsider, I forced my eyes to drag to the garage door.

Hanging from a key hook were the old Buick's keys.

I hadn't driven it—Mom had bought it after her old Jeep died, a few years after I left Bennett Wood. But it would make things easier and, hell, it wasn't like she was using it.

Sighing, I hefted one of the taped boxes in my arms, grabbed the keys, and went out to the garage. The car's door took a little tugging to open and there was a stale, musty smell that hit me the second it was pulled open.

I sighed, gently loading the box in, and then went to the front. Before loading everything, I wanted to make sure that the damn thing actually started.

I sat gingerly on the old seat, the heat nearly suffocating. With both my legs stretched outside of the car, it wasn't impossible, but it *was* uncomfortable.

The car spluttered, the keys sticking a little as I gave it a hard turn, but eventually came to life. The old radio came on, too loud, and I started, jumping in my seat. It was a country music station and I cursed, turning it down with a quick flick of my wrist.

I loaded the car up with as much as it could hold, packing nearly all the boxes in the kitchen.

Driving to the retirement home, I couldn't get the AC to kick on and instead cranked down the window, sticking one arm out as the air flow brought life back to me.

Pulling into the parking lot, I cut the engine. The building looked nice, like it had been recently painted. Mom never had to come here, but we had talked about it a few times in the years before. She might've had to move in if things had turned out differently. I was relieved that it looked nice, even though she hadn't been there.

I grabbed the first box, a smaller one, and headed toward the front door.

And froze, feet stuttering to a stop as soon as I stepped on the sidewalk.

There, a few feet away from the door, bouncing on the balls of his feet, arms stretched out to his sides and shaking, fingers wiggling as if he was prepping for something, stood Joshua.

I cocked my head.

He was facing the door, but the position of the building had it so I could make out his expression.

It was tight, lips pursed and eyes narrowed, and I almost turned around just to give him his privacy. He sighed, looking up at the sky, and his mouth twisted and moved rapidly, as if he was talking to himself.

Aw, hell. I could come back later. I went to turn, but the box slid from my hands and crashed to the ground.

Joshua jumped, his head snapping to me.

Slowly, I bent down to pick up the box. Thankfully, this one was just full of various potholders. Why my mother had enough to fill an entire box, I'd never understand.

"Uh, hi. Hello." Joshua lifted one hand, as if to wave, and then thought better of it and let it drop.

"Hey," I cocked my head, lifting my eyebrows.

He shuffled back and forth on his feet, and then sighed heavily. "Sorry!"

I looked down at the box in surprise. "Nothing broke, it's good."

"I mean—about ducking out on you. I wasn't—I just—felt awkward and it was early—"

I lifted a hand to stop him. He clamped his lips closed. "We both knew what it was, don't worry about it."

Joshua's face relaxed a little, expression twisting from remorseful to something a bit more bashful, and he shrugged one shoulder. I couldn't help the small smile that pulled at my lips.

He was dressed in a similar way to when he had come to the diner yesterday, but the scruff on his face was thicker. His eyes looked warmly over me and memories of last night were enough to make my whole body try to shiver.

He glanced down curiously at the box in my arms, and I shrugged in response.

We were quiet for a minute, Joshua bouncing back on his heels, hands shoved in his pockets. He was looking between the retirement home and me, slow moves of his eyes. Didn't look like he was all that glad to have me there, seeing him outside the doors. I considered asking but the way he was flickering his eyes, teeth digging into his bottom lip, I decided it wasn't really my business.

I cleared my throat and his head snapped up, an expression I couldn't decipher crossing his face.

He smiled. "Um, so, since we're already here—and since I *did* sort of cheat you out of a good morning," he smirked at me and I felt my face heat up, "wanna get out of here?"

I wasn't quite sure what he had in mind, but I did know I very much wanted to go.

A flare of disappointment curled around me and I shook my head. "Sorry, I've got to meet the realtor after this but, uh, maybe after?"

Joshua smiled, stepping forward and closing the space between us. His eyes flickered across me as he pulled a cell phone out of his pocket. "Nice shirt," he commented lightly, a teasing smile still on his face, and then he lifted his eyebrows. "Your number?"

Surprised, I rattled it off. He typed quickly.

My own phone buzzed in my pocket. "That's me," he said, nodding toward where the buzz came from.

"I'll call you," I said.

He laughed. "Text me, old man."

I rolled my eyes at him, mumbling 'old man' under my breath, and then walked into the retirement home, ignoring Joshua's bright laughter behind me.

Chapter 7 - *Joshua*

I ducked out of the way until Jay was gone, unsure of how to explain why I was here. I was grateful he hadn't asked—he had given me a curious frown but otherwise didn't try to question me.

I didn't know if it was because he didn't care or if he was just too used to minding his own business to think it important; either way, I was glad.

But now he was gone, the little beige clunker skirting away, and I didn't have any other excuse. I had half hoped that Jay would take me up on my offer to get out of there, even if all it would have done was delay the inevitable. I didn't want to tell him why I was there and the invite seemed like a good distraction, as well as a delay.

I signed in at a front desk, trying to keep myself from looking around too much. The entryway opened straight into a big room with round tables. A young woman was standing in the middle, holding a small bingo cage. The room looked about half-filled, a few nurses lounging around near the elderly.

Any of these women could be Bernice. Despite ample internet searching, I hadn't really learned much about her.

The nurse at the desk was watching me. She looked like my foster mom, her hair pulled back in a bun and a tired but kind-looking face. She glanced down at the sheet I signed and pulled back in surprise.

"Here to see Bernice?"

"Yes," I said, nodding quickly. "Do you know her?"

The woman smirked. "I know all my residents, yes. I'm the D-O-N here."

I tilted my head, frowning. "The... don?"

"D-O-N," she corrected, setting down the clipboard and coming around the side of the front desk. "Director of nursing."

"So basically you run this place?"

She offered me a wide smile, heading down toward the hallway. "Basically. Now come along," she added when I didn't follow her. I scrambled to catch up. "Why don't I know you? Bernice has been here for a good hot minute."

I felt the sharp pain of skin breaking before I even realized my teeth had sunk into my bottom lip. Hissing softly, I released the pressure. "I—uh, just got to town."

She shot me a look, stopping in the hallway with her hands on her hips. "You wrote that you were family."

Hopefully. Sort of. "Yes."

The D-O-N, as I now knew her to be, narrowed her eyes. "Feel like elaborating?"

"We're—estranged," technically true. "I'm not sure she'll be happy to see me." Definitely true.

The nurse considered for a second before sighing. "Well, okay then."

She continued down the hallway and I followed. Though the doors were all open, I didn't peer into any of the rooms. There was a distinct smell of cleaning solvents and while it wasn't pleasant, I was sure that was the best option.

Stopping at one of the doors, the nurse sent me one last glance before rapping her knuckles on the open door before walking in. "Bernice? It's Janet."

"Janet?" The woman's voice was soft and I peeked in, hesitating at the door. I didn't want to invade the woman's privacy but my curiosity was so potent, clawing at me, it was nearly blinding.

Janet waved me in. I could hear her talking sort of softly with Bernice and I swallowed hard, wiping my hands on my jeans, and then walked into the room.

"This is Josh," Janet said.

"Joshua," I automatically corrected, still gazing around the room. It was small and decorated in a lot of florals, an armada of stuffed animals on the bed.

In a wheelchair parked by the window, Bernice stared up at me.

I felt my mouth go dry. Just a few feet away from me were the answers to all my questions—questions that I hadn't even been able to form yet.

I found myself sinking into an armchair, scooting it over until I was facing her.

Janet was still in the room, one hand possessively wrapped around the back of the wheelchair. I glanced at her and she raised an eyebrow.

Well, then she wasn't going anywhere.

I guess it was a good thing—I was a stranger who admitted to having a complicated relationship with her resident.

Bernice was looking at me, eyes focused, but with a little confusion—she couldn't place me, but I wondered if I looked familiar. If the structure of my face, the color of my eyes, was a Selwyn trait.

My foot bounced, toes tapping against the linoleum floor.

"Hi," I said, after a long minute of silence.

"Hello," she said pleasantly.

I leaned forward in the chair, arms on my knees, hands twisting together. There were moths all inside of me, nerves nearly forcing me to shake.

"I'm, um. Hi. I'm Joshua."

"Joshua," she repeated, her voice clear. She was looking at me but I didn't know if she could tell. Her own face was small and withered, age and a life now mostly indoors creasing her so I couldn't see if we had the same bones, the same blood. She was my family and I was desperate to recognize myself in her.

"I'm here because—have you ever heard of genetic testing?"

She frowned, face scrunching, and after a long, breathless pause, she nodded. "No, sorry."

The words were a surprising contrast to her affirmative nod and I blinked in confusion. I looked at Janet and she just shrugged one shoulder at me.

"Um, okay. Well, basically. Okay. I'm, um. I was, um, adopted, and I found out recently through a genetic test that I'm actually—well. Related to you. To the Selwyns."

Bernice didn't look particularly surprised. "What do you mean?"

"I mean, we're related. We're family."

"No," she said sadly, shaking her head. "I'm sorry, I don't know you."

"I—I know. I know but we're related. I don't really know how, I was hoping you could help with that."

"No, young man, see, we're not related. I don't know you."

I felt my mouth open and close a few times in confusion. I looked at Janet and she was watching me with sympathy now.

"Oh, tell me. Did you start down in the dining room then?" Bernice started to talk about her favorite employees here at the retirement home and promised to put in a good word for me.

"I—the DNA chart told me you were my great-aunt. Do you have any other nephews?"

She cocked her head. "My nephews?" She shook her head and changed the subject.

We chatted for a few minutes, but any attempt at talking about our family connection ended up with Bernice getting confused and changing the subject. After a few minutes, I realized that it wasn't going anywhere.

Janet walked me out. "It's not your fault," she said, sighing. "Bernice is—she has dementia and is starting to fade in and out a little bit."

There was a low lump in my throat, disappointment flaring through me. "Right."

"Sorry, kid."

I thanked her and left the retirement home. Jay's car was still there and I moved quickly to mine so that we wouldn't run into each other again. My whole body was thrumming with sad disappointment and I didn't need to deal with an inappropriately growing crush on top of that.

I sighed. This trip was not going how I planned *at all*.

Chapter 8 - *Jay*

I was halfway through packing up the living room when the realtor rang the doorbell at three on the dot.

I wiped my hands off on my jeans, giving the messy, half-packed room a once-over, before sighing and opening the door.

Sarah Larson looked exactly as she did on her website. Her hair was pulled in a severe bun and she smiled sunnily at me. "Mr. Richardson?"

"Yeah. Uh, Ms. Larson?"

"Yes," she confirmed, lifting her neck to look around me.

I stepped aside, waving her in. She peered around, eyes narrowing at the ceiling as she swept through the house. I followed her, awkwardly shoving my hands in my pockets.

"You'll need to fix this," she pointed to a water stain on the ceiling. I followed her finger and frowned at the damage that I hadn't noticed before. She then gestured toward the appliances. "Update all of these, of course. No new homeowners are going to bid even near asking if you have these eighties-style appliances. Does the stove even still work?"

I fought back the urge to glare. "Yes."

"The foundation looks good—I'll have an inspector come in sometime soon, of course." She then stalked through and I followed behind.

"Oh, this," she made a disgruntled sigh. "Have to repaint this, fresh coat for the whole room actually." I followed her eye line and felt a distinctive ping of despair, which I immediately shrugged off, at her annoyance. The living room did look a little faded, I guessed, but the doorway had the tiny marks of my height, from when I was just a kid, all the way through high school. Repaint. Fresh coat.

I scampered to keep up with the realtor when I realized she'd left the room and was listing the things wrong with the bathroom. "Gut this, the whole thing honestly. This sink? Way too small. Is this the only bathroom?"

After nearly a half hour and minimal interaction, she lead me back to the kitchen, leaning on the island.

I looked around my apparently very lacking house. "I didn't realize so much was wrong with it."

Sarah smiled kindly. "It's a good house with good bones, but for the best sale, you'll need to get the house in order."

I inhaled deeply, fingernails digging into my palms as I clenched my fists. There was a low throb behind my eyes, just a tick of frustration building beneath my skin. I didn't want to *fix* the house—I wanted the house gone.

Being here in my old house, being in my old town, reminded me of all the things I didn't have— would probably never have. A life on the road didn't exactly lend itself to mortgages and picket fences. And hell, where would I go even if I did up and quit my job, or somehow find someone who didn't mind me being gone for days on end? Here? Bennett Wood? Surely the place hadn't changed so much high school—if the names weren't enough, the disgust from the ones who heard the rumors about me, the distinctive lack of other gay men my age would be a real downer. I mean, sure, besides a few short visits secluded here at Mom's, I hadn't been in the town in twenty years, but that didn't mean it was all of a sudden a safe haven. I wanted a house of my own, a life of my own, one off the roads and away from the never-ending *go* that had been fueling me for years.

I ignored the pang in my chest and pushed the thoughts away. It didn't help me any to dwell on things that I couldn't change. At least not right now.

"I'll get them fixed," I told Sarah. She was scribbling on a clipboard, taking notes of the other things to change.

"I'll email you," she said, reaching out to shake my hand.

I thanked her and showed her out, watching as she climbed in her car and drove away.

It wasn't quite four, the meeting had gone by quickly, but my stomach was clenching painfully as I remembered how little I had to eat today.

I pulled out my cell phone, grabbing a glass of water, and decided to text Joshua.

He had given me his number after all—and as used to eating meals alone as I was, there was something about this day, packing my mom's stuff for charity, a hefty list of household projects to complete, a sense of complete frustrating dread thick in my gut—I just didn't want to eat alone if I didn't have to.

Not to mention the small but growing part of me that *wanted* to see Joshua. He was— interesting.

I shot him a text quickly before I could change my mind, quickly plugging my phone into the charger and taking a lap around the house so I wouldn't just stand there, waiting for a read message to pop up.

I was sweaty again, the day's heat sticking to me, and I could use a shower—especially if I was to see Joshua again.

My phone buzzed, the light trill sending a shot of adrenaline straight through me.

Free whenever. Dilly's??

The grin that pulled at my lips was too broad, a bit embarrassing in its eagerness.

You been to Balto's?

Balto's Pizzeria was a staple, the best place to get pizza in a forty-mile radius. I hadn't had it in decades and even just considering it had my mouth watering. I really hoped Joshua didn't have a problem with it.

After a few more texts, we agreed to meet at seven.

After packing up a few more boxes, I threw in the towel for the night. I ended up spending longer in the shower than I thought I would, cursing when I stepped out and saw the clock. I brushed my teeth quickly and shaved as carefully as my speed would allow. I got dressed, grabbed my phone, wallet, and keys, and left the garage with five minutes to spare.

Joshua was standing outside of Balto's when I got there, thumbs hooked in his front pockets. He was leaning against the brick wall, a few feet away from the door, and his eyes widened when he saw me. He lifted his hand and waved lightly.

"Hey," he said, kicking off the wall and meeting me at the edge of the sidewalk.

"Hi," it was early enough that the streets were still fairly empty.

Joshua pulled open the door, waving me in with his free hand, and I squeezed between him and the wall, my breath catching in my throat as we brushed against each other.

I stepped into the pizzeria, nodding at a waitress as I led us over to a booth. It was in the front corner, a little secluded, and most of the other patrons were in the back of the restaurant.

Joshua slid in the booth in front of me, head craning as he looked around.

Balto's was decorated like an old cabin, black and white photos hung up on the walls. It hadn't changed a bit since my high school days.

The waitress came over and took our drink orders. I asked for a tea and Joshua asked for a Coke.

When the waitress flitted away to grab our drinks, Joshua picked up his menu and flickered his eyes across the options. "What's good here?"

I shrugged. "The pizza."

His lips quirked and he rolled his eyes. "Cheese?"

"Pepperoni," I corrected. "Best in town."

He mimicked my shrug, smiling lightly. The waitress dropped off our drinks and we ordered a large pie with pepperoni.

When she went to put the order in, Joshua grabbed a napkin and fiddled with it, his fingertips shredding the thin paper. His eyes kept sweeping across the room and I could feel his leg bouncing under the table.

I couldn't tell if he was nervous or if this sort of energy was just how he always was.

I wasn't nervous, per se—I was just *aware* in a way that I normally wasn't. So much of my life was second-nature, muscle memory of driving hard through the night, meeting deadlines, sleeping in discount motel rooms until the next job started. I wasn't the kind of man that went on *dates*—if that even was what this was.

But something about Joshua made me want to try, even if it was doomed from the start.

I cleared my throat, delighting in the way his head snapped up, and ran my hand through my hair.

"How was the realtor?" Joshua asked suddenly, voice a pitch too high. He winced and I grinned at him.

"Uh, it was—good." I swirled the straw in my drink, shrugging. "Apparently, there's a lot wrong with the house."

Joshua's nose scrunched up as he frowned. "Wrong? Like? It's falling apart?"

"Aesthetically." I snorted. "I've got a whole list of things I have to fix before the realtor wants to put it up for sale."

"And you didn't want that?"

I shook my head. "Hell no. I thought I'd be here a week tops."

"That sucks," he sympathized, hands curling around his glass.

"It's fine," I said automatically. I realized I had been complaining and quickly shifted gears. "How was your first full day on your trip?"

Joshua's teeth sunk into his bottom lip. He chewed on it slowly, his face drawn in concentration, before letting it go with a pop and shrugging. "It was fine. Got myself a nice setup at the campsite across town."

"Oh, that's good," I said, trying to withhold my slight surprise. He didn't look like the camping type, but he was young—younger than I was really giving him credit for, probably. Saving a few bucks made sense. "You do any sightseeing?"

His lips twitched. "What sightseeing is there to do in Bennett Wood?"

Good point. I shrugged, thankful that the waitress interrupted my line of questioning when she came by to drop off the pizza.

Joshua was staring at it hungrily. "Dude, that looks *good.*"

I laughed. "It will be."

He grinned at me, grabbing a slice quickly and taking a huge bite. I watched him with wide eyes, laughing as he winced and started fanning into his open mouth. "Hot, hot, hot."

"That was not your best move."

He rolled his eyes at me, blowing carefully on the slice before taking another bite.

I shook my head at him, transferring a piece of pizza onto my plate and letting it cool away from the heat of the pie.

"Get everything dropped off at the retirement home?" he asked, taking a sip of his Coke.

I cocked my head. "Mostly. I've still got a few rooms left to pack."

He hummed around a mouthful. "You're not keeping anything?"

"Some," I said. "But—you know—" I shrugged.

He nodded.

"Why were you there anyway?" I asked, finally picking up my slice. I took a bite and nearly groaned—Balto's really was the best.

Joshua had fallen silent and I looked up, surprised. He was fidgeting a little in his seat, picking at a pepperoni.

I nearly backtracked and apologized. "Lis—" I clamped my mouth closed when he started to speak.

His words came out, a little rushed, and I took another bite to keep me from saying something that ruined it. "I was visiting someone—a relative. Distant."

I waited, eating quietly as he considered. He was looking at me with a hard expression before nearly melting, leaning across the table, his next words coming out in a tumble. "Honestly, it went so badly. Like, beyond badly. Terrible."

"Wasn't happy to see you?"

"No," he slumped down in his chair. "It's just—she didn't even believe me."

"Believe you?" I wasn't keeping up.

His eyes snapped to mine and his lips pursed, narrowing into a thin line as he considered.

I couldn't stop myself from mirroring his position, my own body leaning forward. "I know you've got things you aren't saying," I said slowly, dipping my chin until I caught his eyes. They were the same bright hazel that had knocked the wind out of me in the diner. "You don't have to say nothing to me. But, ya know. You can."

Joshua's face softened, lips twisting to one side of his face—he was so expressive. Even as he tried to avoid telling me things, even as I knew there were things I didn't know about him, he couldn't stop himself from sharing bits of himself in his every expression.

When he decided to tell me, I could see it in the way he leaned back, tongue darting out to swipe across his lips, and the small look of relief. "It's—I'm not here just for a road trip. I mean, I am—a little—but also I came to Bennett Wood with a purpose."

I grabbed a second slice, nodding to Joshua to show I was listening, but trying not to interrupt him.

He continued. "I, uh, don't know my birth family. But I found out, sort of recently, that they're from here—from Bennett Wood. And, uh, since I had some time, I thought I would come and—you know. Try."

"And one of your relatives was at the retirement home?"

His foot was tapping beneath the table and his fingers tore at a napkin, shredding it with his long movements.

"Yeah," he sighed. "She just—didn't even believe me that we were related. And I don't really know what to do from there, I really thought she'd, like, be my ticket in."

"You couldn't just show her what you had?" I assumed he had *some* sort of proof if he was all the way here.

He shrugged. "Dementia. The nurse told me after that it was unlikely she'd even remember meeting me."

Despite the casual tone he used, his whole body seemed to curve more into itself, his expression crestfallen.

The urge to reach out and comfort him was surprising. I placed my hands in my lap to stop myself.

"I don't know. Maybe I shouldn't even try to reach out to any of the other Selwyns. I don't—I don't know."

I perked up. "Selwyn?"

"Yeah," he tore off a piece of crust and popped it into his mouth. "Bernice Selwyn, that's who I went to see."

"Oh! I—I can help."

Joshua's eyebrows shot up. "Uh, okay, you're a nomad trucker."

I rolled my eyes, struggling to wipe my smile off my face so I could try and glare at him. "With serious roots in the town."

"Despite your best effort," Joshua added.

I laughed. "I know the Selwyns. I—it's been a bit, but they'd remember me. I could introduce you."

Joshua pulled back, leaning hard against the linoleum booth. "I, uh, I can't ask that of you."

He looked uncomfortable. I tore my eyes away. "Not askin'. I'm offerin'."

I gave Joshua a minute, going back to my meal as he considered.

"I—can't accept something for nothing," he said, shaking his head.

I raised an eyebrow. "I bought you dinner last night."

"And you got my delightful company," he teased.

I rolled my eyes. "And I get it again now. Can't that be enough?"

Joshua rapped his fingers against the table, looking at me hard, his eyes squinted. Then he grinned and snapped his fingers. "I'll help with the repairs and stuff."

"What?"

"Your house," he explained. "I'll help with that stuff you have to do, the repairs and stuff. In exchange."

I cocked my head.

For a pretty nice and open guy, there was a part of Joshua that seemed unwilling to accept help. He was untrusting, unwilling to let the balance be thrown off at all.

I couldn't help but wonder what happened to him that made him like that. From what I knew, twenty-two-year-olds didn't usually have a hang-up with accepting help.

"Sure," I said, realizing that I hadn't said anything. He brightened and my own lips twisted to match his grin.

"So I guess that means I'll see you again?" he asked, voice pitching a bit lower as he leaned in.

I pushed my empty plate away, arms on the table as I hunched forward to meet his whisper. "I guess so."

His eyes sparked, and I could barely catch my breath. He was fascinating, in a way that was altogether mesmerizing.

His head turned just a little, and I couldn't look away from the sharp line of his jaw and cheek.

Joshua's eyes caught mine again and I felt my face heat, flushing. "Want to get out of here?"

He looked around and shrugged. "Sure," he said, and then waved our waitress over. I paid quickly, ignoring his attempt to reach for the check. He shot me a look and I shrugged half a shoulder. As much as he seemed to hate handouts, we both knew he was tight on money. The least I could do was pay for the pizza.

After tipping the waitress, I threw the leftover pizza in a box and handed it to Joshua.

He tucked it under his arm and I opened the door, letting him out first.

"So, uh." He stopped a few feet away from the door. "I'll text you tomorrow?"

I blinked in surprise. "Uh?"

"For the house stuff. I've got time, obviously, so we could get started tomorrow if you want."

"That'd be great," I admitted. The sooner, the better.

"Then my car's over there. Back to the campsite." He offered me the pizza box.

Still surprised, I just shook my head. He shrugged, offered me a smile, and then jogged over to his car. I watched him unlock it and slide in. He leaned out the window, a wide, lopsided grin on his face, before driving away.

Disappointment flared in my gut that Joshua was going back to his campsite instead of home with me, but I guessed two nights in a row was a lot to ask. And as much as I'd hoped to spend more time with him tonight, I was already looking forward to hearing from him tomorrow.

Chapter 9 - *Joshua*

The sun had just set as I drove back out to the campsite, stopping along the way to pick up a few bottles of water and bug spray. The site let me rent a tent from them and I had a few things packed in the trunk, anticipating I'd be staying in less than good digs.

Even though he hadn't come out and asked, I knew that Jay had wanted me to go back to his place with him. His surprised expression when I said I was leaving had me fleeing quickly before I'd change my mind. Now that I was walking through the darkening wood, I was starting to regret my decision to not go back with him. The cool house, the big, comfy pull-out bed—I bet that Jay even would make some good tea or coffee. Something warm and comforting.

Warm and comforting, sort of like Jay's eyes—the care in them had been nearly debilitating. Jay was a quiet man, soft and careful with his words when he did use them. We hadn't talked much during dinner, but it was still clear that he was affected by my presence, the way I was his.

I didn't want to be affected in any way.

It wasn't that late, barely scratching nine by the time I undressed and got settled in my tent for the night. But my days in Bennett Wood were weighing on me and my eyes felt heavy, even if my mind was still whirling.

My tent was secluded for the most part, but close enough that I could still see the main parking lot if I got out and peeked around the tree line. It was close enough to the main road that I didn't have to be afraid of anything, but far off enough that I wouldn't, like, stumble into another camper.

I couldn't stop thinking about the way Jay had felt the other night.

My body was still sore, my muscles aching from the workout I'd gotten wrapped around Jay's thick frame. His chest was broad, narrowing a bit in his hips, but not so much that my thighs hadn't quivered separating far enough for him to fit. That, mixed with how hard he'd fucked me. I had been a mess before he'd even gotten inside of me, which was probably a good thing—his cock had been so big, thick and fat, only growing harder and harder as the night went, that I could imagine it would have hurt something sharp if I hadn't been so goddamn desperate for it.

Even just thinking about it now, the way his face scraped against mine, his hands pressing hard enough to bruise into my skin, his sharp gaze—I could feel myself growing hard in my pajama pants, my cock stirring with interest as I considered the way that Jay had felt. I shifted, uncomfortable, and tried to think of something else.

I succeeded in not remembering the other night—

But only because now I couldn't shake the images of things we *hadn't* done, things we could have been doing right now if I hadn't been such a tired idiot.

Butterflies leapt in my stomach, my whole body nearly thrumming alive.

Without really meaning to, my hand reached down and slid into my sweats. I was half-hard already, my stomach pooling with heated interest, and I decided *fuck it,* pulled the sleeping bag over me, and closed my eyes.

My hand curled around my hardening dick, the feeling of my coarse, dry skin making a small hiss slip from between clenched teeth. I pulled it back out, licked a long, wet stripe, and slid it back beneath my pants.

Ah, I groaned. *Much better.*

I closed my eyes, imagining what we would be doing if I was at his house.

I imagined the couch as it was when I first went into the house, the bed tucked away. The light streaming in from the closed curtains soft, barely there, just enough to see the sharp planes of his face, the curve of his lips and jut of his hands as they curled around his knees in anticipation.

I imagined Jay in just his boxers, already tented and a wet patch growing, his broad chest bare and his face pink with warmth and excitement.

I twisted my hand, the pad of my thumb scraping against the head of my cock, and I imagined myself settled between his legs. Thick, warm thighs pressing against my arms. I was shaking, would be shaking. I imagined the way his thighs would feel against my hands. I would hold on, fingers digging a little to hold myself steady. No—one hand on his thigh, the other reaching up farther, fisted on the couch to hold me really, firmly steady.

I'd wait a minute—his cock would be dripping, fat drops of precum sliding down the head, over the thick ridges, but he'd hold himself steady. If his thighs weren't shaking underneath my hand and his cock wasn't a pretty, blushing red, I wouldn't know how bad he'd want it—Jay would lock his muscles into place and keep his expression clear, though his pupils blown wide would give him away.

I'd kiss the sensitive, pale skin between his thighs, open-mouthed and wet, little bites that he'd suck a deep breath in through clenched teeth, over and over again, unrelenting with my careful kissing, never getting where he really wanted me.

I'd wait until he couldn't stop himself, hands finally fisting in my hair, and he'd drag me over to where he wanted me. It would burn just a little, too hard, too fast, and I'd have to quickly open my mouth wide to swallow around him.

He'd taste *good*, warm and heavy on my tongue, and as soon as I wrapped my lips around him, he would let out that sweet groan of approval.

I imagined the way my throat would feel, full of him, my tongue and lips working fast. I imagined winding a hand down my own body, wrapping around myself, and when I imagined that, I tugged hard on myself, hips stuttering off my sleeping bag for a minute as the heat was washing over me.

"Just like that," I imagined Jay saying, his voice thick in a drawl. I lifted my hand and imagined it was Jay's, siding down my cheekbones, down my jaw, to gently pull my chin down, thumb tugging on my jaw to open my mouth wider. "Fuck, sweetheart, so good for me."

The sound of the nickname, even as it was just a memory spilling back into the forefront of my mind, was enough for me to lose my grip and without much warning, I was spilling over my clenched fist, hips canting forward as my orgasm washed through me.

I groaned, muffling the sound with my clean hand, trying to keep any other campers from hearing what was going on. My release spilled over my hand and wrist, staining the inside of my pajama pants. Grimacing, I used the material to clean myself off as best I could before carefully sliding out of them and tossing them to the corner of my tent. Now that my body was relaxed, sleepiness was starting to take over.

I sank deep into the sleeping bag, sighing heavily, thoughts of a gruff, handsome stranger lulling me to an early rest.

— — — —

The next morning, I woke up with a crick in my neck, a sore back, and a naked lower body. I frowned down at myself before memories of last night hit me and I glanced over at my filthy pajama pants. Well, that was a bad decision.

I dug around in the duffel bag I'd thrown inside of the tent until I found clean underwear and slid them on under the covers. I still had on my thick socks and a t-shirt, so I dressed myself enough to unzip the tent, letting in the fresh morning air and stretching.

There were no more tents or cars than there were last night and I offered up a quiet, thankful prayer that I hadn't inadvertently scarred someone with my late-night activities.

I stretched, wincing at the sound my back made when it popped, and then quickly got dressed. I would need to do laundry soon. I was in the same jeans as yesterday and a short sleeve blue t-shirt. Hopefully, the darker shade would hide any sweat that gathered from helping Jay with his house.

I was a little excited—as much as I should have been dreading manual labor, the idea of seeing Jay again, especially after last night's thoughts, was pretty appealing.

After tackling my teeth and face in the small camping bathroom, I packed up around my tent the best I could, checking that I had my wallet, phone, and keys before jogging the short distance to my car. I unlocked it and slid in, immediately cranking the windows down to let the stale air out.

I plugged my phone in the lighter jack, making sure it was starting to charge, and then headed toward town.

It was early still, only just past seven, but the sun was blaring and I was in high spirits.

I stopped off at the little cafe, Mountain Bakery, I had noticed yesterday, unplugging my phone to text Jay and ask if he wanted anything.

He hadn't texted back before I ordered so I got us two large black coffees. I was bringing them back to my car when I saw he had texted me his order—large black. I grinned.

When I got to Jay's, I parked by the ditch, ignoring the excitement building in my stomach. I was just—glad, to have something to do, a lead on my bio family—it wasn't *just* about seeing Jay.

Still, when I rapped my knuckles on the door, I had to consciously stop myself from bouncing on my feet and grinning.

"Hi," I said, as soon as the door swung open.

From his spot halfway behind the door, Jay blinked at me.

With his hair sticking up and a slight pillow crease on his cheek, Jay's eyes went wide and he tugged on the dark blue bathrobe he wore. I couldn't help but look him up and down—he was in fuzzy black slippers. Rumpled and creased, he looked like he had just rolled out of bed. My chest clenched painfully.

He was *frigging adorable.*

This time, nothing was stopping me from grinning wide at him. I offered him his coffee and he reached forward, jutting one shoulder in front of the door to hold it open without his hand, and greedily took a long gulp.

"Tired?" I teased.

He raised his eyebrows, giving me an unimpressed glare. "You're early."

I ignored the flare of guilt. "I texted."

"Mmm," he grunted, stepping aside. I walked into the house.

The last time I was here, I wasn't necessarily paying attention to the colors and knickknacks. Now, though, it was obvious that this wasn't Jay's place. The whole thing was brimming with old lady vibes.

I sipped at my coffee, politely not noticing how goddamn *strong* Jay's chest looked from where his robe was parted. He was just in a pair of short gray boxer shorts, his thighs bare and tanned, the muscles there thick.

Flashes of my fantasies last night came back, remembering the way I imagined his thighs feeling around my face.

I looked away fast, feeling my face burn as I hid behind my coffee cup.

Luckily, Jay seemed too tired to be paying attention to me. "I'm gonna go get dressed," he muttered, his voice low in a raspy drawl. I imagined it was the first time he spoke all morning. I nodded, still avoiding his gaze.

I moved around the house slowly, taking in the small framed photos in the living room that were still unpacked. The kitchen had been empty and the living room half packed up. I imagined there wasn't much more.

"So," he came back quicker than I thought and I jumped a little. Coffee sloshed out of the lid and burned my hand.

"So," I repeated, wiping my hand on my jeans. I looked up and Jay nearly blinded me.

He was in another tight white t-shirt and light wash jeans, the knees a little worn but otherwise in good condition. His hair was a little wet and I imagined him splashing water on his face to quickly wake up.

"Thanks for the coffee," he said, cheeks tinting just lightly, a small smile pulling at his lips. As I was drinking him in, my eyes hungry for the shade of his jaw and the turn of his lips, he was drinking me in, too, his eyes appreciatively scanning me.

I tried not to preen under the attention.

"Wanna get started?" I asked, trying to divert his attention from my clearly growing desire.

He was sufficiently distracted and nodded, shoulders slumping just a little as he looked around the room. He took another long drink of his coffee and I mimicked him, mourning a little that mine was already half gone, and we set them on the fireplace's mantel. He had shoved the bed back into the couch but blankets were peeking out.

We moved around each other easily, Jay handing me boxes and newspapers while he started in on the books on the far shelf. He didn't say anything else and I tried to relax in the quiet. Jay wasn't one for needless words and I liked that about him—he brought a sort of soft, peaceful energy out in me that I normally didn't notice.

I went to the knickknacks and started to gently wrap them in newspaper. There were an alarming number of blue jay figurines. Some were glass, others metal. There was a crocheted pillow with a fat little blue jay in the middle. I looked around the room and noticed a few other holding this motif. There were probably more hidden away in the boxes Jay had already packed.

I held a small glass blue jay in my hand, my thumb rolling over the curves and bumps in the design. It was intricate and looked hand-painted. It was really beautiful.

"That's—" Jay stopped, cleared his throat. "Um, that's my mom's."

My first instinct was to say: awww. My second was: no shit.

I decided to just glance over to him and see if he'd share anything more.

"She collected blue jays. All sort of them. It was, well, frustratin' at times," I could hear him fighting off a bit of a laugh. He was still packing books, not looking at me. I looked back at the figurine in my hand. "Throw pillows, decorative plates, hell, mugs—anything that had a blue jay on it, she had to have it."

I waited and he didn't say more. I gently wrapped the bird up. "Is that where you got your name?"

He froze, just a split second—if I hadn't been watching, I wouldn't have noticed the slight way his face crumpled, his eyes closing, his shoulders tightening. In a split second, it was gone, and he was shrugging, loading books into a box and then taping it shut.

"It's beautiful," I said, after a beat, going to lower it in the box.

His head snapped up and Jay stopped me with a half-raised hand. I froze, watching as unexpressed emotions flickered across his face rapidly. "Let's just—leave that one out."

I nodded, careful in my unwrapping, and placed it securely at the back of the shelf.

Jay didn't say more, and neither did I. I knew that whatever he was feeling was big and I mostly couldn't believe that I was allowed to be here.

Jay glanced over at me, face still open, and he offered me a very small smile. My chest flipped and I smiled back, falling into the sweet, gentle quiet.

Chapter 10 - *Joshua*

The rest of the morning was spent in that same sort of quiet gentleness that I hadn't felt with anyone other than Jay. It was just—peaceful. I attributed it to his age, maybe. He was just a quiet person but he was also a good guy. I had only known him a couple days, but I was sure that he was. I could feel it. Growing up in foster care, I had fine-tuned my ability to read people. It was a vital part of survival for a while. Proved true again and again, and I knew that it was true now. Jay was good.

We packed the rest of the house pretty quickly. I finished up the living room, except for the few items that Jay had pointed out that he wanted to keep out, and he'd tackled his mom's bedroom. Apparently, it was mostly cleaned out anyway. We dropped the boxes off at the retirement home. I followed in my car, so we wouldn't have to take two trips, but Jay offered to carry them all in. I knew it was so I wouldn't have to go in, and I probably ought to have just ignored the gesture and helped. Instead, I sank lower into my seat and sent him a grateful smile.

Helping Jay pack up his home felt like a double-edged sword. On the one hand, having something to do physically, a way to distract myself and busy myself was good. It was more than good—felt like purpose, even if it was just packing knickknacks. On the other hand, I couldn't help but feel the sharp pangs of sorrow, of jealousy, of something, when I watched the delicate way Jay handled his mother's belongings. The clear adoration he had for her, even when it was shown in nothing more than a softening expression. He missed his mom, but he had a long time with her. My mom—well, I didn't have a house or knickknacks to remember her by.

Still, it was too hard to hold onto that feeling for more than a few minutes at a time. Jay was too kind.

Jay asked if I wanted food, since other than another few cups of coffee while we packed, we hadn't eaten and it was nearing two o'clock. But the nerves in my gut were too filling and I shook my head.

We had decided to drop off my car at his place and drive together to Dr. Selwyn's. Jay had called ahead and told him he'd be stopping by. The man, Jay had assured me, sounded surprised but not unhappy by Jay's little visit. He didn't mention me. I didn't know if that was a good idea or not but in the end, I was going no matter what. I had to at least *try*. Might as well not give them the shot to turn me down.

The sun was beaming in through the window. I had one arm out, fingers tapping nervously on the little beige door. This car was a bit of a joke, nothing more than a cassette player in it, and I wished we were in mine instead. At least I had an aux cord.

My stomach rolled.

Jay shot me a look but, true to form, didn't say anything. He just drove slowly and steadily along the winding roads, driving a little bit outside of town.

When we pulled up to the house, I could barely see the structure—nerves and awkward dizziness were starting to get to me.

What was I thinking? Just showing up here and being like, hey, yeah, we're related. People didn't just *forget* about babies. What if this was some matter of infidelity or crime or painful teenage decisions or—I didn't want to cause problems for anyone.

Jay was already out of the car and opening the door for me. I nearly spilled out of it and he quickly reached down, hand curling around my elbow to straighten me. My hand fell on top of his and we caught each other's eyes.

I pulled away, fingers burning, and thanked him quietly.

Jay cleared his throat and led me up the path. The house was big, white, a full display of Southern wealth. Rosebushes lined the front of the house, pristine. I felt wrong even just stepping on the porch. He knocked on the door and I sucked in a deep breath.

Here goes nothing.

I didn't want to cause problems but I also wanted a family. I squared my shoulders and exhaled deeply.

The door creaked open and a tall man in a nice charcoal gray suit stood there.

"Jay!" He said pleasantly. He opened the door all the way and reached out, shaking Jay's hand. He looked—prim. Proper. Like a stand-up guy. I knew that he must have been, being a doctor, but it was still weird to see this guy who was maybe related to me, looking like he was worth a million bucks. The man's long face shifted, eyes that were the exact same shade as mine softening, and he clasped his second hand around Jay's. "I was so sorry to hear about your mother's passing."

Jay cleared his throat and nodded. "Kind of you," he muttered.

Dr. Selwyn glanced over at me curiously and I lifted one hand, waving a bit awkwardly. With my other arm, I lightly elbowed Jay.

He jumped a little and shot me an exasperated look before smoothing out his expression. "Doc, this is Joshua. We were hoping to have a little chat with you and the family." Still looking confused, but now distinctly curious as well, Dr. Selwyn gestured for us to enter the house.

I followed behind them, trying not to eye the family portraits on the wall or the expensive decor. It was all just—so different than where I was from. Foster homes didn't have a bowl full of—was that just? glass? crystals? What the fuck?

I stumbled into Jay's back, not noticing that they had stopped walking.

A woman with light blonde hair, curled and pinned to her head, walked into the room. She was wearing a yellow sundress and looked the pinnacle of the Southern wife. She looked between us all and then crossed the room quickly, heels ticking off the floor, and gathered Jay's hands. There was another woman in the room, looking at me with sharp, curious eyes.

"Oh, little Jay. Your mother was such a bright spot of this community. She always brought the *best* pecan brownies to church."

Jay's face was red now, but I knew it was with embarrassment, not emotion. I hid my snicker behind a cough.

The woman spun to me. "And who is this?"

"Josh," Dr. Selwyn said, coming to his wife and placing a hand on the small of her back. "He's here to talk with us."

"With us?" she repeated in surprise, eyes flying to mine.

"Uh, Joshua," I corrected automatically. "If you have the time, that is."

"Of course," Dr. Selwyn said smoothly. He gestured toward the couches and Jay and I sat on one. Dr. Selwyn took the other, and looked at his wife. He started when he saw the other woman, clearly having forgotten she was there. "Coffee, Patricia? Oh, you remember Hanna, don't you, Jay? She's Patricia's oldest friend. Comes for tea, what, twice a week, isn't it?"

"Now, Doctor. Don't call me old." She turned to Jay with big, expectant eyes.

"Uh," it was clear he didn't. "Of course. Hello."

Hanna sat on the only chair and smiled. "So nice to see you again, dear."

"Patricia," Dr. Selwyn said. "Coffee?"

"Oh, of course," Patricia darted off, assumedly to the kitchen. The doctor turned to us, a sheepish smile on his face, his hands out as in *wives, what can you do?* It was clear he had no idea he was talking to two gay men.

I glanced at Jay from the corner of my eye. Actually, I didn't know if Jay was gay—I mean he was a little gay. Gay enough, obviously. I made a mental note to maybe ask Jay about his sexuality later. Older guys tended to be a bit—prickly about that, though, so I would have to brace myself for some biphobic bullshit just in case.

This was all beside the point.

We all waited awkwardly. I knew that Dr. Selwyn was deferring to Jay and Jay was deferring to me and I had no fucking idea where to start.

Patricia came back with a tray of coffee. It was in a nice ceramic pot with empty cups. "Luke is right behind me with cream and sugar."

My chest twisted—Luke Selwyn. He was the other relative I'd found in town, the one whose social media I had checked out. He was supposed to be my brother. My chest twisted.

My hands shook when I reached out to take the coffee that Patricia offered me.

"What a nice day for visitors!" Patricia said, clapping her hands together as she settled next to her husband. "First Hanna stops by and now Jay and his mystery guest. A nice day, indeed."

She tilted her head up, smiling wide at Jay. "Ah, please, help yourself—there's more coffee in this house than we need!"

Glancing over, I saw he had already emptied his small cup. Jay's quiet "thank you, ma'am" was punctuated by Luke coming in with a second tray. I had to tear my gaze away, busy drinking in his face to see if it looked like mine.

"Uh, hi," Luke said to Jay.

Jay smiled politely, but subdued.

"Join us, if you'd like," Jay extended the invasion that was fighting on my tongue. Luke looked at his parents but then shrugged and sat next to his mom.

My feet were bouncing, knees knobby as I drank my coffee, looking around the living room without actually taking anything in.

"I'm afraid I still don't know why you're here or why you've brought young Josh with you," Dr. Selwyn said with a rueful tone.

"Joshua," Jay corrected automatically and a little bit of my nerves fell away. I wasn't here alone, but I also wasn't here with my friends, the people who would be able to see me fall apart. Jay was kind and good, but also still virtually a stranger. It emboldened me.

"I, um. Okay. This is going to sound, well, nuts, or maybe not nuts, but it's going to sound—something. For sure."

Luke's eyebrows were raised and he leaned forward a little, interested in the gossip, and Patricia's eyes narrowed. She looked sharp then, her pleasant exterior melting a bit.

Hanna just looked thrilled. I tried to ignore her.

"Uh, anyway. Um." I looked over at Jay helplessly. He didn't smile, not exactly, but his eyes softened, his head tilting just a little bit to the left, and I took a deep breath, exhaling slowly. "I don't know where to start."

Patricia smiled kindly. "How about the beginning?"

Good point. "I'm, um, a foster kid. I mean, I had a family, for a bit, but they were an adoptive family, and then, you know, *after*, foster. Which isn't bad or anything, I mean—" it was bad, a lot of the time, but that wasn't the point. I was getting ahead of myself. "Anyway, I just graduated college, and my friends, they, um, they got me this? DNA test thing? It's—you spit in a tube and mail it off and I think the government now, like, owns my DNA or something but—"

Jay cleared his throat. He twisted, feet shifting until the toe of his boot knocked lightly against the heel of mine. I exhaled slowly.

"We're—family. Somehow. My DNA results said I was biologically related to the Selwyns. I went to see Bernice but she—didn't really get what I was saying, honestly. And so, I thought. I'd come here and just, you know. See."

Patricia had leaned into her husband, a hand on her chest. Dr. Selwyn was looking at me with a pointed, dark look, his lips tightly pursed and his eyes narrowed.

"That's *impossible*," Patricia said, vehemently. She shook her head. "Absolutely impossible, isn't it?"

"It is. Impossible," Dr. Selwyn said just as forcefully.

I could feel the fluttering in my chest that had nothing to do with nerves and more to do with hesitant, crashing disappointment. My gut churned.

"I—I can show you the results—"

"There's no need," Patricia said coolly. "We are quite a small family and there's absolutely no way you're related to Bernice."

"And Luke," I said. The guy's head popped up, his expression halfway between shell-shocked and angry, and I sank further into the couch. "The results had you by name."

"I have no idea whose child you might be, but it's certainly not anyone of ours. We would know if there had been a *baby*."

I knew my mouth must be open, having felt my jaw drop, but there was nothing I could say.

"His—*your* name was on my sheet, man! We're related." I told Luke, hoping he'd at least acknowledge it.

"How would they even *know* that?" Dr. Selwyn said, his voice quiet and thunderous at the same time. It was a dark sound and I shivered.

"I—I was helping Auntie Bernice with some research," Luke stammered, looking between his parents. "Back when she started forgetting things. It was just a dumb online test thing."

The database had both of their DNA. I knew that Luke *must* have believed me.

"My name is Joshua Matthews. If you look at your profile, you'll *see.*"

He narrowed his eyes—hazel eyes, the same eyes that his dad had, the same eyes that I had— and though it was small, barely a dip of his chin, he nodded.

"You need to leave," Patricia said. She looked at her husband for support.

My breathing was all fucked up and my eyes were stinging and I couldn't tell if this was hurt or anger or—

Jay stepped in, standing quickly and putting both of our cups on the coffee table. I had forgotten I was even holding mine. "We'll go," he said. Though his words were appeasing, I could see the crease in his forehead, hear how there was no kindness in his tone.

Patricia nodded shortly, turning away from us, and I let Jay reach down and tug me up. He led me out of the house, the quiet, furious whispering of the family that refused to claim me playing us out.

Chapter 11- *Jay*

I was buzzing with anger when I marched Joshua and I out of the Selwyns' house.

I didn't know what I expected, but for them to be so—dismissive of Joshua really wasn't it. It was rude and mean and—and—downright *inhospitable* of them to treat the kid that way.

He had come all this way, put himself out there. And if the DNA said they were related, I was pretty damn sure they were related.

I hadn't known the good doctor to ever be such a dick before.

I shook my head, unlocking the car and opening the door for Joshua. He got in silently, grabbing the handle and slamming it shut before I managed to close it.

I knew he had to be upset—he'd looked like a fish out of water for most of that conversation and I could imagine two rejections in a row were likely to sting a little too fresh.

I got in the car, quiet, and drove us back to my place. Joshua's car was still parked there. I hoped I could convince him to come inside, maybe get some food. He hadn't eaten at all today, as far as I knew, and I was getting hungry, too. Maybe there were more Selwyns we could find.

I gently reached out a hand and set it on top of his. He stiffened but slowly, incrementally, relaxed under my touch. He flipped his palm and intertwined our fingers. I could feel how he was shaking.

He dropped my hand and unbuckled when we pulled onto my street.

When I pulled up in the driveway, I turned to ask Joshua about dinner, but he was already out of the car before I had unbuckled.

I scrambled after him, but he was already halfway to his car. He looked *pissed*. His shoulders were set, jaw clenched, and he had his keys in his fist so tightly that his knuckles were white.

"Joshua."

He didn't slow down. I half-jogged to catch up. He was already at his car.

"Joshua. Josh, hey." I reached out one hand to his shoulder.

"Don't call me that," he snapped, spinning around and leaping out of my touch.

"Sorry," I pulled my hand back. He was glaring at me, chest heaving up and down, and I was afraid that anything else I said would spook him. His whole body was locked tight.

"Whatever," he said, after a minute.

"Do you want to come inside? We could get dinner and—"

"No." He turned to the car, fumbling with his keys.

I moved to lean against the back door, bending a little so I could catch his eye. "Joshua, come on—"

"I said no. I don't want to go into your house or eat your food or talk about our feelings or anything."

My eyes widened and after a minute, I let his harsh tone roll off my back. "That's fine," I said, trying to keep my tone even. "I'm sorry it went down like that."

"Whatever," he said again, more forcefully. He yanked open his door.

I shot out an arm and stopped him from getting in the car. "Look, Joshua—"

"No!" He turned to face me fully. The way we were standing, our chests were nearly touching and he had to crane his neck up to see me. His cheeks were pink and his eyes glossy, but there was complete, righteous anger in them.

"Sorry, I just—"

"Just what?" He poked my chest. "You don't know me! Listen, thanks for the introduction, thanks for the ride, but you *do not know me.* We're not friends. We're—you were just a quick fuck and thanks for that but now if you could just get out of my goddamn business?"

His voice was venomous, spitting his words at me. My heart hammered in my chest, my whole body feeling void of blood or oxygen, but I stood my ground. My expression didn't waver.

I knew that he was just lashing out, that he was in defensive mode, but *fuck it*, if everything he said wasn't also true. It stung.

He was still glaring at me, but we could both tell the heat was draining from him. He was hurt and embarrassed and he wasn't one to let others in. I hadn't known him long but I did know that.

"Can I please go?" he asked, voice losing some of its steam.

I stumbled out of his way, stepping back into the yard.

Joshua muttered out a hard, biting *thank you,* and then climbed into his car. He turned it on and sped away quickly.

I watched the car until it turned off the street, disappearing into town.

Fuck. I headed into my house.

The day had started off so good. He'd been there with coffee and a smile and he'd moved around my mother's house like he liked it, like he fit there. It was easier to breathe when he was there. We had talked. Not a lot. But a little—enough.

Being around Joshua had felt—easy. Simple. *Good.*

But I had been an idiot to try to comfort him like that. He had clearly been upset and, hell, he was right. What did I owe him? Nothing. We were just strangers who had conveniently helped each other out. He didn't owe me his life story—though the bit about his past he had told the Selwyns was seared into my memory—and I didn't owe him any comfort. It was an arrangement. And it was over.

I kicked off my boots and undid the button of my jeans, not bothering to turn on the lights. There was beer in the fridge that I had picked up the other day, and I opened one, leaning against the counter as I took a long pull. It was cool and entirely earned after the day I'd had.

How long had I even been here? Too long. Too goddamn long in this small town, in this small house. Here, I couldn't hide behind the quiet comfort of the road, the anonymity of nothing permanent, the inability to form any sort of connection. It had been two days and I had felt more for Joshua than I had for any other guy in a decade.

It was this town. It was getting to me.

This was why I didn't get involved with guys so much younger than me. They were—volatile. Emotional. And with Joshua, it was all too easy to forget what we were: namely, nothing. I shouldn't have stuck my nose in his business. Should have just introduced him to Doc and then slipped out. But I hadn't because I was *curious* and feeling protective over his smaller, shaking frame.

I groaned and took another drink.

I was an idiot. But at least I wouldn't make that mistake again.

Chapter 12 - *Joshua*

I got two blocks down the road before the regret settled in.

It wasn't Jay's fault that my birth family didn't want anything to do with me. It wasn't his fault that I was a *child*, incapable of dealing with my emotions without lashing out. It wasn't his fault that I was completely incapable of accepting his comfort in any way, especially when it was so goddamn apparent that I didn't deserve it at all.

God, I was so stupid. Coming all the way here, asking for attention and recognition, and, what, fucking *validation* from the family that tossed me out in the first place?

God. Damn. It.

I drove around the block three times, trying to decide if I should go back to Jay's. He deserved an apology. He deserved me to leave town and just leave him out of my bullshit.

The more I drove, the less angry I got. Well, the anger was still there, but a lot of the raw, aching pain was gone. I was being dramatic. I knew this was an option and it stung like *hell* but it happened. This was all I could do.

Now that my adrenaline was fading, I was starting to get exhausted. I considered going straight back to the campsite and just going to bed, but I hadn't eaten yet today and there were still a couple of things in town I needed to do.

I drove through a drive-thru, grabbing a quick meal, and ate it as I drove through town. I wasn't quite sure where the building was, but after finishing the food and driving through the town twice, I ended up parking out in front of the County History Museum.

I went inside, still sipping at the soda that came with my meal. The museum was small, dedicated to preserving the memory of the small Western North Carolina county that Bennett Wood was in, and I found myself lost in the history, stuck on the town's thorough description of its residents. Genealogies, from the founder of Bennett Wood, driving down all the way to the current mayor; I'd cry nepotism if the man didn't look so cheery in his display.

"Excuse me," I jumped a little at the voice. A small woman with gray hair and a thick purple sweater tapped on my plastic cup. "No drinks in the museum."

I flushed. "Oh, man. Sorry." I looked around and she helpfully pointed at a small trash can by the door. I darted over, sucking a long drink, and dropped the cup in. "Sorry."

"You said that," she said teasingly. I couldn't help the small snort that came out. She grinned. "I'm Maggie. The curator here."

Maggie wasn't a day under sixty but looked like a bright, happy woman. I shook her offered hand. "Joshua."

"Why are you at my museum, Joshua?"

I looked around. The place was nice—I had been to a lot of museums in my life. They were usually free and a way to spend time in the nice air conditioning without anyone trying to mess with you. Growing up, that was important. In college, it was a brief reprise from studies or friends when I needed a moment to myself. I could feel myself starting to relax in the familiar atmosphere.

"Just, you know. Stopping by." I waved a hand.

The woman might have been older, but she wasn't any bit less sharp. Her eyes narrowed and she hummed. "People don't just stop by the county museum, young man."

"I disagree," I didn't really.

Her lips twitched. "I thought you might. Let me show you around."

I followed her as she pointed out each object—old documents that were yellow in the corners, black cursive ink bleeding into each letter. Photographs and early newspaper clippings. Though the museum *was* small, it took Maggie nearly an hour to talk me through the items, what they meant. Some, she explained how she obtained them. Apparently, she'd been the curator for two decades, having grown up in the county when she was just a little girl.

It was easier, almost like being back at college in a lecture, to let the woman's voice wash over me.

"Now," she said, leaning against the wall. "I've given you *my* story. What's yours?"

"That's hardly a fair trade," I was amused by her nosiness. I couldn't help it, she was such a bubbly person. Maggie shrugged, unbothered. Words were in my throat, trying to come out, even though I knew that anything I shared with her had a good chance of getting around the whole town. Still, I wanted to talk. And it wasn't like I could just call my friends—it was too much, too confusing, too little—and I couldn't go and talk to Jay.

Fuck, I was only going to be in town for another day anyway. With the Selwyns not wanting anything to do with me, I didn't have anything to stick around for.

"I just had an argument, I guess, it wasn't really a fight, with—this guy I've been seeing," I rolled my eyes at how high school I sounded.

"That's upsetting," she offered.

I shrugged. "My fault. I—he was just being nice and I wasn't very nice in return." I turned and looked at a piece of art on the wall. Apparently, it was in the first ever mayor's office. It looked, well, bad. It was ugly. I became immediately fond of it and took a quick photo of it to send to the group chat.

"Are you going to leave me in suspense?" Maggie demanded.

I laughed at her. "Sorry, sorry, it's—just. Okay, so I was really mean to him when he was just trying to be nice to me but we're not even like, seeing each other, we're just. I don't know. It's casual, it's just a fling, but I still feel bad. He was just being nice."

"Why were you so upset?"

I realized that the sixty-year-old Southern woman just brazenly went past the "gay fling" and straight to the heart of the issue and my heart swelled for her a little.

"I—uh, oh, fuck it. I came to town to meet my birth family. I got some DNA results so I know it's them but they just completely rejected me. Said that there was no way I was one of them. I mean, I shouldn't have been surprised. I guess I wasn't. I mean, I figured already that my biological family didn't want anything to do with me. After all, that's usually the result of not being with your biological family in the first place, right? And, you know, it isn't like anyone else wanted me. So I really don't know why I thought they would be different—they're all the same."

The words all tumbled out in a slurring mess, spilling out from my lips before I could even consider it. I felt my face heat up in embarrassment.

Maggie was nodding, though, a serious look on her face as she considered my story.

They were all the same. But in a way, Jay wasn't the same. He *was* different; a little bit, at least. He cared about me. Maybe not much. But a little bit. He'd sat with me at the Selwyns' place, brushed his boot against mine in solidarity. He'd tried to comfort me, talk to me, when I was upset.

It was more than I could say for most people in my life.

"Your man?" Maggie prompted.

I shrugged, shoving my hands in my pocket. "He was there when I met with them, and I was, you know, angry. And Jay tried to talk to me but I just—couldn't, you know. He was being kind and I was shitty."

Maggie hummed a little, nodding at me. "You should go apologize."

I winced. "Well, yeah," she was right, of course. But—just—going back to his place? I had been such a dick. He didn't want me there.

I stared down at a scuff mark on the floor, considering. I guessed I could text him. He was old as hell but had been texting me pretty well so far. He must be able to handle the nuance at least a little bit.

I don't know. Maybe that was a bad idea, too.

"I'll think about it," I told her.

Maggie smiled and reached out, patting my cheek affectionately. "Good boy."

"Thanks for—all this," I said, waving an arm.

She grinned. "The museum's always open."

"Really?" I couldn't imagine that was true.

She laughed a little. "Metaphorically. Actually, we're closing soon, so." She gestured to the door.

I laughed, heading out. "I can catch a hint. Thanks again, Maggie. I'll think about what you said."

"Let me know how it goes," she called after me as I left. I offered her a wave and jogged back to my car, surprised at how dark it had gotten. There was something nice about Maggie's museum, the same as there was about Jay's house. Something that didn't hurt to be around. It was nice.

A small, fleeting part of me was already aware that I was going to miss it when I left.

Chapter 13 - *Jay*

I had settled on the couch with my second beer, Mom's ancient television playing some sports with bad coloring. The night was still young, my body still filled with the nervous energy of the day. I had slept more since getting back to Bennett Wood than I normally did in a week on the road.

Part of me missed the road. Missed my truck, the crackling of the radio, the way it felt to be mindless and efficient for twenty hours a day.

The other part of me was already mourning leaving this place.

I had spent so long running away from Bennett Wood, from stability, from the life that I thought I'd never be able to escape, that I never stopped to consider what life I was actually living on the road.

That flare of desire, the stupid desire for something *more,* something firm and real, was back again. It felt like a twisting of the gut, like a sore chest. Like homesickness, even as I sat firmly pressed in the home I'd grown up in.

The place was nearly all cleared out now. I'd be back on the road before I knew it.

My cell phone ringing broke me from my thoughts. I groaned, setting the beer on the floor and pressing my hands on my knees to lift me up. My back cracked when I stretched, padding into the kitchen where my phone was plugged in.

The realtor's number was on the screen.

"Hello?" I answered, clearing my throat when the tone was a little gruff.

"Hi! This is Sarah Larson."

"Hi, Sarah." I went over to the fridge, pulling it open. There wasn't much in line of food there.

"I have someone interested in the property. Even *before* it's fixed up. I know you weren't exactly excited about the idea of doing some work so I figured we should jump on this as best we can."

"Uh, great." I didn't know why she had to call me at six o'clock to say this, but sure.

"I know it's late but they just got off work." Sarah continued. "They want to do a walk-through now."

"Now?" I looked around the place. All the boxes had been taken out. Besides furniture and a few little items, it was mostly empty.

"If that's all right."

"Uh, sure. That won't take too long?"

"We'll leave right now. Maybe a half hour, hour tops."

"What do I do then?"

"It'd be best if you went out for a bit, honestly. New buyers don't like to feel watched."

"Right," I glanced down at myself. "I'll, uh, leave now."

I cleaned up quickly, turning off the TV and taking the beer bottles to the trash. I slid on shoes and my flannel, taking the trash with me to deposit in the garbage can outside.

I grabbed my keys and got in the truck. I didn't realize until I was halfway down the road that I had chosen my truck instead of Mom's car. Driving it even without its trailer was second nature to me and for a few minutes, I let myself get lost in the gentle thrum of the engine.

I parked in the far lot of the Whole Foods, and hopped out of the truck. Glancing at my watch, I made a note of what time I'd left so I would know when I was allowed to return.

The grocery shopping cleared my head. I just bought a few things—more coffee, some milk, bread, eggs. A pack of lunch meat and a case of bottled water. I drove the cart through the deserted aisles of the grocery store, losing myself to the monotony and quietness.

I wondered what it would be like living here again. After leaving at eighteen, I was so sure I'd never come back, that I'd never settle down. But that scratching urge was clawing its way through my chest more and more nowadays. Not here, necessarily. But somewhere, maybe.

I'd barely been out of my house since I got back, it felt like. Moving through the store with just a few other locals grabbing their midweek meals was—relaxing, almost. The domesticity was nice.

A flash of tan skin and brown hair grabbed my attention, the figure moving into the next aisle before I could get a good look. Without really meaning to, I pushed my cart into that aisle, following.

The guy glanced at me and then went back to his cereal choices.

My face burned and I quickly grabbed the first thing my hand touched and then went to the next aisle. I had—

God.

I had thought it was Joshua.

I was blushing hard, barely paying attention to where I was pushing my cart now. I had thought it was Joshua and I had darted after him like a lunatic. What would I have even done if it *had* been Joshua? He didn't want to talk to me. He had made that very clear.

I knew that he had been upset, that the disappointment of the Selwyns' reactions were weighing on him when he lashed out at me. He probably wouldn't have been so harsh or unwilling to engage if it wasn't for that. I clung to that, trying to squash the urge to flee. Even my fingertips were itching, desperate for the feel of the steering wheel.

I wanted to run. But more than that, I really wanted to not want to run. I felt all shook up, a soda can about to explode. I wanted to be there for Luke, even as my instincts begged me to run.

He had just looked so *sad*, really devastated. He had been so nervous and all that stuff about his past, I hadn't known. He'd put himself out there and that family had just ignored him.

I didn't know a lot about what he'd gone through, but I knew that he didn't accept help easily and was quick to fold into himself. Watching that vulnerability be ignored was—infuriating.

I had wanted to make things better. I had forgotten that wasn't my right.

The whole fling was a mistake, maybe. I shouldn't have started something with someone so young. I was here, back in Bennett Wood, cleaning out my mother's house—for weeks now I had been fighting back thoughts of stability and home and a new life beyond what I was living right now. It was stupid of me to think those things would mix well with a fling with a young guy. Barely out of college, he was here on an *emotion-driven road trip*. I never should have gotten involved, no matter how attractive he was.

I paid for my groceries, unable to stop myself from scanning the lines. I didn't even know who I was looking for. Old classmates? Neighbors? Joshua, even though it was a terrible idea? I was just—looking.

After taking the groceries to the car, I pulled out my cell. It was still early—I'd killed twenty minutes but not much more than that.

My truck was far enough back that there wasn't anyone else parked near me. I made a quick sandwich with the materials from my bag and ate it slowly, leaning against the rig. I chewed slowly, realizing how hungry I was as I finished it. I made another and ate that just as slowly.

Thirty minutes.

Aw, hell. Whatever.

I drove back to the house. Sarah had said that it would take about a half hour. Hopefully, they would be gone.

There weren't any cars and I let out a breath of relief. I grabbed the bags with one hand and held my keys in the other, assuming Sarah would have locked up on her way out.

The door, though, was cracked open. I sighed, pushing the door open and letting it close quietly behind me. Luckily, the door opened into the kitchen and it was clear. I heard shuffling from the bedroom.

"We could paint it yellow," I heard a woman's voice, light and happy. There was low chuckling and then, *"Yellow would be nice, honey."*

More shuffling. I put away the groceries and tried to ignore the chattering that was coming from the couple, now apparently in my childhood bedroom—it had been cleaned out years ago and was used as storage, until Mom passed. The woman talked about turning it into a nursery. The man suggested they change the windows and add beams to the ceiling.

They were small cosmetic changes, in the grand scheme of things. No worse than the changes Sarah had wanted me to make, anyway. But still—the bedroom didn't *need* beams added to the ceiling. Sure, sure, a can of paint, I got that—but adjusting the structure? It was unnecessary.

I slammed the fridge harder than I meant to.

"Honey, if we just break down all of this, just demolish it completely, we could start fresh."

Starting fresh. How many times had I wanted just that? A fresh start, something new. Hell, three days ago I probably would have agreed that knocking the whole place down would be better. Now, it felt like ants on my skin when you went camping. Like I was itching and being chewed on.

"Oh, maybe an add-on. Is there room for that? This place could be bigger."

Oh, hells bells. I tugged harshly on my hair.

I couldn't stand there and listen to them and decided a nice walk around the block or two would be better than hearing their plans for ruining my mother's home.

This is what you wanted, I reminded myself. I kicked at a rock in my way, trying to remind myself over and over again that I didn't care if the house got changed. I didn't care if it got demolished. I was selling it—I was selling it and getting the hell out of Bennett Wood again. This was what I wanted.

It's just—

This house had been my home base my entire life. Even when I didn't want to be there, it wasn't like the place didn't not want me back. Mom always made sure that it was a safe space, a good space. My mom grew up in that house, had all but died in that house—my grandfather had *built* the house with his bare hands. It had been in my family for two generations and—

And now the second bedroom would be yellow.

That wasn't a bad thing. This was what I wanted.

Wasn't it?

Chapter 14 - *Joshua*

I sat outside on a log by the lit bonfire outside of my tent. The fire pit hadn't been used so far for my trip, but as soon as I got back tonight, I had lit it. It wasn't cool out and I didn't have any s'more materials, but it was still early when I got back to the campsite and I needed something to do with my hands.

I could practically feel the way my posture was dipped, feel how curved in on myself I was. I imagined Griff mocking me and then demanding I go to yoga with him.

I felt incrementally better when I was at the history museum. Maggie had been a pleasant surprise, a nice woman with good advice and kind eyes, but the farther I drove from her, the more I realized her good advice was just, like, common sense I was refusing to acknowledge.

I knew that I needed to go and apologize. Jay had been really nice to me and I had been a dick. Jay had rolled with the punches but I had seen the look on his face—he'd been hurt. His whole expression had fallen and I just—fuck, I felt bad.

But it wasn't like I had been lying, I guess. We *were* nothing to each other—except, that was only true in the technical sense.

Something about Jay had wormed its way into my head and now all I could think about was what I colossal mistake I'd made.

My birth family had rejected me. They had denied my existence, even as I sat there in front of them. But like I'd told Maggie, that was—mostly expected. But Jay had never been like that. He'd been kind and considerate and accepting of me since we'd met. And then he reached out when I needed it, when he knew that I needed it, and I'd rejected *him*.

I had to go back. I had to do the right thing and apologize, even if all that happened was he slammed the door in my face and refused to forgive me for being so rude. It would be fair but he still deserved an apology.

And even as I braced for it, a small part of me was arguing that, hey, Jay might not do that. Maybe, just maybe, Jay wouldn't shove me away like everyone else had.

I decided firmly, putting out the fire. I wouldn't blow Jay off, even if we weren't meant to be anything more than a fling. We were—something.

I took a deep breath, inhaling deeply, exhaling slowly, and then got back to my car.

The sun was setting, the skies starting to darken as I drove back to town. My fingers drummed against the steering wheel. Was I ever going to *not* be nervous on this trip?

It started raining as I pulled up at Jay's house. I looked up at the sky and hoped it wasn't an omen. I jumped out of the car, ignoring the pelting rain. I jogged up to the door, knocking on it a few times too many to not be eager.

By the time the door opened, I was absolutely drenched; my t-shirt was plastered to me, my hair flat against my forehead. I was shaking and I had no idea if it was because of the rain or the nerves of having the door slammed immediately.

Jay appeared behind the door, his eyes wide. He looked me up and down, jaw falling open.

As soon as I saw him, I could feel my heart rate steady. I was grinning before he said a thing.

"Joshua, what the hell?" His mouth was opening and closing like a fish out of water.

"I—had to see you."

Jay's eyes widened impossibly, comically larger. I waited, trying to keep my shivering at bay, while he assessed me. The rain was pouring. A bolt of thunder interrupted our silence and I jumped.

Jay finally seemed to realize that it was pouring and he frowned, glancing at the sky, before stepping aside. "Come in."

I ignored the reluctance in his voice the best I could, even as my stomach fell.

I knew he was angry. I just—had hoped.

I stepped in, looking around. The place looked good all cleared out. Still needed less floral wallpaper but what could you do.

Jay left me alone in the kitchen silently. I watched him go, wincing at the cold shoulder. It was subtle, compared to his normal casual quietness, but I could feel it. I slowly toed out of my boots and smiled thankfully when Jay came back with a towel for me.

"Thanks," I muttered. He nodded, leaning against the kitchen island.

I toweled off the best I could. My shirt and jeans were still sopping and creating quite a puddle on the kitchen floor. I ignored it, hoping that Jay would, too.

He glanced down at the floor and then back to me. Damn.

"Why are you here, Joshua?"

I fought against the distinctive urge to fidget. "I—I'm sorry."

Jay didn't say anything more, but his face relaxed just a little, as if he had been preparing for me to be mean again. Guilt flared at that.

"I lashed out earlier, and you were just being kind. I'm—shit, man. I'm sorry."

Jay's head tilted, eyes narrowing just a little, as he considered my apology. It wasn't a great one, I knew, but—I didn't know what else to say. I was just sorry.

"Take a seat," he said finally, nodding toward the table. "Want a beer?"

"God, yes, please."

He froze at the door and his eyes shifted to me. "Are you even old enough to drink?"

My head snapped up in surprise. A laugh burst out of me at his horrified expression. "Yes, yes. I *am,* thank you very much. Want to see my ID, officer?"

"Shut up," he mumbled, grabbing the bottles from the fridge. When he came back to the table, his cheeks were pink.

The chair was uncomfortable with my wet, heavy denim, but I was too grateful at Jay's apparent forgiveness to offer any complaints now.

He handed me the beer and we sat silently drinking for just a moment. "I am sorry," I said again.

One small corner of his lips lifted. "Yeah." Then, after a brief pause. "Thanks."

He didn't seem upset but the guilt in my gut was still there.

I owed him more than just a haphazard sorry. I owed him an explanation.

I looked down at the table, rolling the bottle around in my hand. I started to tug a little at the edge of the beer's label.

"I, um. So, you heard, earlier, with Dr. Selwyn, um. So I had a family, a really nice family, when I was just a kid. But then there was this accident—car accident. And my parents died. I was eight. I know that they weren't my biological parents now but, you know. That's beside the point."

I glanced back up at Jay, feeling a little bit winded, and then started tugging more at the label, watching the way that the beads of sweat dripped down the bottle's neck.

"Anyway, after that, I got put into a bunch of different foster homes. Some—were fine. Others were less. I—it was shit, you know? And it was a long time before I met anyone that, like, gave a shit. That I could trust. Maybe college. But even then—I mean I love my friends, but you know."

"You have a hard time trusting people," Jay surmised.

I sighed, unable to keep my eyes from flickering back to his. "Yeah," I mumbled. "It's just—the foster homes were crap and I just don't really know how to deal with people, well, not treating me like crap."

Jay's hand closed over mine, the contact a little surprising. I jumped even as I leaned into it. "It's okay."

"It's not," I could hear how low, how quiet my voice had gotten. I pitched forward. "You've been so nice. Nicer than I deserve. And I just—it's not an excuse, my shitty childhood, but, like, earlier with the Selwyns, I just—I hoped. I shouldn't have, I should have had realistic expectations of all that, but I couldn't help it. I hoped. And then it all just came crashing down on me."

"What did?" Our chairs were closer now.

"That I'm just—not wanted. Not really. And, and—" I kept talking over his splutter of protest, not wanting to hear the pitying response. "And then you were really nice and it was just all too much. Again, not an excuse. I just—thought you deserved an explanation."

Jay was watching me, the look in his eyes ineffable. "Thanks for telling me that."

I sighed, leaning forward. I felt—lighter. Better. "Thanks for listening."

He smiled at me, and then recoiled a bit. I frowned at his sudden change in demeanor. "What?"

"You're still wet," he said, as if just now noticing that I was drenched. I couldn't help but laugh.

"Uh, yeah. Where have you been?"

His cheeks were pink again. A blush on a grown man should have been stupid, but it was—well, honestly, it was adorable.

"I'm sorry," he said, standing up. "I'll get you something to change into."

"Oh, you don't—" I stopped myself. "Actually, yeah. Thanks."

He offered me a wide grin before darting into the living room for his duffel and I tried not to notice the way my chest constricted, my heart spasming at the spread of his pretty, soft smile.

This—this was new. The excitement, the lust, the steadfastness of a friendly, good person; that, I recognized. But this, this cocktail of more, of things that I couldn't name but knew were so real that they couldn't be faked—this was new. These feelings that Jay's soft smile evoked were feelings I had never felt before.

He glanced back at me, eyes squinting just a bit from the effort of his smile, and I heard a sigh fall from my lips.

Then I pulled myself up, eyes widening.

Oh, no.

I was screwed.

Chapter 15 - *Jay*

I gave Joshua a pair of sweatpants and a muscle shirt to change into. He thanked me and darted off into the bathroom to get out of his wet clothes.

I thought over what Joshua had said. His apology was sincere and learning more about his past made all of his actions make a lot of sense. He had been hurt so many times—told he was unwanted time after time by the people who should have been there for him.

As surprised as I was to see him at my door, and as unsure as I was about where we stood, seeing him put himself out there had really affected me. It was easy to see how hard he was trying. Joshua didn't owe me anything—we were just two ships passing in the night, really. But he had taken the time to come and make sure I understood and he had shown me vulnerability when it was hard for him to do.

I was angrier now than I had been earlier, though. How dare Dr. Selwyn just throw Joshua out like that? He had put himself out there, really tried, and they had just—tossed him out.

I could see it in his eyes, how little he thought he deserved. He was—such an amazing man, had been through things that made him hard but not jaded. He had every right to not be kind and yet, here he was, offering an olive branch to someone who didn't really matter in the long run.

If Joshua would let me, I wanted to show him that he *was* wanted. That I noticed him, that he was a good man that deserved good things.

Joshua came back into the kitchen, his wet clothes in his arms. He was swallowed by my sweats, having rolled the waist band and the ankles a few times over, the white muscle tee hanging off his smaller frame.

His hair had been towel dried and stuck up everywhere. His cheeks were a bit red and his eyes were wide and bright.

He was *devastatingly* handsome in the warm, soft light.

I shifted in my chair, a bit uncomfortable. I nodded to the garage door. "Dryer is out there."

He mumbled a quick thanks and quickly padded out. I listened to the sound of the ancient dryer being pried open, the vibrations filling the house quickly. He came back and closed the door softly behind him.

"Thanks for these," he gestured to himself.

I waved him off. "Of course."

Joshua smiled. He looked softer now. He came over and sat in the chair at the head of the table, scooting it across the floor until it was facing me. He grabbed his beer, lifting the bottle to his lips. Slowly, he let his head fall back, just a little, and tipped the opening of the bottle into his mouth. Beer trickled out and down, a droplet falling to the corner of his lips and sliding down his chin. He set the bottle down on the table and swiped at the droplet with the pad of his thumb, absently sticking his thumb between his lips to suck it off.

I watched the whole thing, enthralled, my own fist tightening around the base of my beer.

He looked *good* in my clothes. Something was rumbling in my chest and it was hard to focus on, hard to feel or identify, beyond the express desire to feel it *more*.

He ran the pad of his finger around the mouth of the beer, a soft whistle filling the space between us.

His shoulders were broad; they were decorated with freckles and moles, dipping down into his arms a little. Our knees brushed. I hadn't realized I had scooted closer.

Joshua's teeth sank into his bottom lip, his head tilting to the side in a silent question. His eyes were wide, framed by dark lashes. Spreading his legs, he dropped his hands to the middle of the seat of the chair. His fingers curled around the wood there, his body leaning forward into the small space between our bodies. The back of his knuckles brushed against my bare knee.

Each move, each exhale that brought his chest closer and closer to mine, was too innocent to not be calculated. He was toying with me—a game that I was losing. I didn't mind to lose; I just wanted to play. I was glad that he thought of me for the game in the first place.

I reached between us and folded a hand over his. He froze at the contact.

Is this against the rules? I tilted my head.

His teeth released his bottom lip with a pop. He swiped his tongue against the red swell. *No rules.*

Good. I let my gaze fall to his lips, watching as they spread into a wolfish grin. My own expression was surely matching.

I didn't know which of us closed the space, but then one of my hands was behind his head, fingers curled around his neck, and our mouths were crashing together.

Bright, sharp need stabbed through me—thousands of tiny needles, starting in my lower gut, running up my chest and down my legs. My fingers and toes were full of pins and needles. Joshua's skin was pure electricity, lighting me up from the inside out.

His mouth parted just slightly, his tongue tracing my lips, flattening against the roof of my mouth, teasingly tasting my tongue as I chased his. His lips were hot, plush, hard against my mouth, his whole body rolling as he tried to get closer and closer to me. I let go of his hands, and immediately his fingers were entwined in my hair. Joshua was off his chair in a split second and crawling into my lap, his legs winding around me. I wrapped my arm around him to keep him there.

I ran my hand up the back of his shirt, fingernails dragging enticingly down his bare skin. He shivered, moaning into my mouth, fingers tightening in my hair. He rolled his hips, the hard press of his erection bursting against me. This time it was my turn to groan, hips stuttering up to reach his in complete instinct; Joshua swallowed my groan and bit my bottom lip.

I was a mess already. I was wrecked. His lithe body pressed hard and tight against mine. He let go of my hair momentarily to aggressively push the bathrobe off my body. It fell in a pool at my waist on the chair, trapped by my body, and then Joshua's hands were roaming everywhere. His fingernails lightly traced my collarbone, dragging up my neck and holding tight on my jaw before tracing down my neck and shoulders, following the lines of my muscles down to my wrists. He tore his mouth away from mine, both of us gasping for air, our chests heaving, and as he caught his breath, he slid his fingers in my hair, tugging my head back *hard,* and he attached his mouth to the pulse point at my neck.

He sucked hard, tongue and teeth worrying at the sensitive skin there. He left hot, open-mouthed kisses along my neck, tongue swiping salaciously. I could feel my hips canting up, my body tightly strung as I struggled to keep us on the chair. I was already hard, feeling my cock throb, trapped between our bodies.

He pulled my head back again, his face hovering above mine. His eyes were blown wide, cheeks bright pink, lips parted as he breathed heavily. "Jay," his voice was *wrecked,* catching on his exhale.

My cock twitched and his eyelashes fluttered, thighs tightening around me when he felt it.

Fuck.

I secured my arms around him and lifted us both, grinning at his surprised yelp.

He tightened his legs around me as I attached my lips to his neck, loving the way his head fell back automatically, baring himself open for me. I paused in the doorway, leaning Joshua's body against the wall, sliding one knee between his legs, and continued my assault on his neck. I was careful about bruising him, but lavished him until he was writhing between me and the wall, words spilling from his lips as he clenched his eyes closed and his fingernails dug painfully in my shoulders. I could feel his hard cock through the sweatpants he wore, the damp patch rubbing against my stomach.

When all he was managing was the circular rotating of his hips and my name over and over again, my own body helpless against his soft, grunted plea, I secured him again in my arms and carried him the rest of the way to the bed.

I laid him down gently this time, grinning at him.

Joshua was quick to push himself up on his elbows. He lay there, panting. One leg was over the bed, foot planted on the floor, his legs spread far. His sweatpants were tented and wet with his desire, his shirt pushed up to the middle of his stomach, his collarbone and neck pink and red and wet.

He was a goddamn *sight.*

"God*damn.*" I breathed out.

He flushed, glancing down at himself, before back at me. Though he was grinning, it was smaller, his eyes wide with something besides lust—

I remembered my mission. It wasn't just to feel every inch of Joshua's skin, though that was certainly a close second—it was to make Joshua feel wanted.

I grabbed a pillow off the makeshift bed and set it on the floor, gently sinking to my knees. He tracked my every movement, breath catching in a soft *"Jay"* when he realized what I was doing.

Grinning up at him, I tugged at him until his legs were on either side of my body, slowly reaching up and pulling the sweats from his hips. He lifted them up and I pulled the pants off of him, gently lifting his feet until I could toss the pants to the side of the bed.

Bare from the waist down, Joshua curled down a little, and his hands fell to my head. "Jay," he said again.

I looked up at him, questioning. His breath hitched and then he nodded, just once, small, but enough.

I wound an arm around his waist, grinning at the short sound of surprise when I yanked him forward to the edge of the mattress. His legs fell apart further, and I used my other hand to run up and down his thigh. Goosebumps rose where I touched. I looked up at him, catching his eye, as my hand got closer and closer to where he wanted me without ever touching. His eyes were wide, pupils blown, and his breath was coming out in short little pants the more I worked him up.

I let my fingers slide slowly and purposefully across the thick bushel of hair at the base of his cock, slowly trailing one finger up just a half inch, before pulling away completely and digging my nails into his thigh. He groaned loud, eyes falling shut as his face twisted in frustration.

I waited, wondering if he would break, but then he sighed. The tendons in his neck were tight and then he released a long sigh and opened his eyes.

Well, then.

I leaned lower and ignored the satisfied expression on his face. I placed soft, wet kisses at the inner corners of his thighs, gently biting and soothing with a swipe of my tongue, all around the base of his cock. I was gentle, letting my tongue swipe again and again at his thighs and the tight skin near his balls, but fully ignored his cock.

After just a few minutes of this, Joshua let out a low whining sound, canting his hips up to try and push my face where he wanted me.

I grinned into his leg and kissed gently before lifting my gaze again. Though he still looked half-blown away, it was clear that frustration was working its way into his expression, too. His abs were trembling, his whole body held tight as he fought the urge to take care of himself. His cock was long and rock-hard, the shaft a bright red and the tip an angry plum, leaking precum down the curves.

He was young and hard and *desperate* for something I was withholding.

My mouth went dry—the urge to reach out, to wrap my lips around him, let my tongue slide across him to swipe up that delicious droplet was nearly all-encompassing.

"Jay, please," he begged.

It was musical. I looked up at him and the image before me was too good—it was *breathtaking.* His face was sweaty and red, his chest heaving, his whole body trembling with utter want. "Please," he repeated.

"Please what?" I was teasing him.

He huffed out a half laugh, his head falling back. "Jesus Christ."

I leaned over him, my hot breath blowing a little on the tip of his swollen cock. "Not good enough."

He moaned, long and loud, cock twitching desperately as it felt my heated breath. I grinned.

After a minute, Joshua stopped muttering to himself and said, "Jay, please, *fuck*, please touch me. Please."

I shivered. His voice was chocolate and coffee and everything good in the world. I had to reward him. I had to give him what he wanted, now that he had asked.

I reached out, placing my hands on either side of his hips, and slowly licked a long stripe from the base of his cock to the tip, catching the beads of precum dribbling down. His answering moan was loud, gasping and full of breathless air.

I wrapped my lips around him, slowly lowering myself until he was fully planted in my mouth, the tip of his cock brushing against the back of my throat. I stilled, feeling him throb inside of me, until I got used to the feeling and then softly sucked, harder and harder until he was gasping, his moans now guttural, pulled from his throat and gut and his hands were in my hair.

"Jay, Jay, Jay," he chanted. I licked and sucked at him, bobbing my head up and down to keep his cock firmly in my mouth. When I got to the top, I swiped my tongue against the slit, grinning around my mouthful when I tasted him. "Fuck!"

When he started lifting his hips up to meet my every move, his whole body tight, legs drawn taut as he fucked up into my mouth, I added my hand, fingers curling tightly around him. It was wet and messy, my spit spilling from my lips, dripping down his cock to coat my fingers as my hand tightly jerked up and down.

His eyes were clenched shut, mouth open, as his hips lifted and fell in rapid movement.

I pulled off completely, thumb swiping over his head, and he let out a strangled cry, and then stilled in my hand. "Fuck, fuck, *Jay!*" he cried out, fingers *tight* and painful at my scalp, his hips frozen halfway lifted from the bed, and then he was coming, hard, spilling down my fingers and the side of his cock. I bent down as I realized it was happening and wrapped my lips around his messy head, licking and gently sucking to get what I could out of him. He was babbling, incoherent pleas mingling with his moans.

When he was spent, his body crashed onto the bed. Gently, I licked and mouthed at him until he was clean and then pulled off, looking up at him.

He was leaning on his elbows again, his expression open and *helpless* as he watched me. "Jesus Christ, Jay," he said.

I licked my lips and his eyes, impossibly, darkened.

He glanced down at me—his cum was spilled all over my fingers and hand, a little bit dripped onto the boxers that I was straining against. He tore off his tank top and handed it to me in offering.

I could feel my face warming and I bit the inside of my cheek before shaking my head. He tilted his head, eyebrows furthering, but now that my task was over, all I could think about was how little blood there must have been in my head. My own poor, neglected cock was *straining* against my boxers, painful in its hard twitching and I slid my hand in, feeling some of the sticky wetness grab on the material of the cotton boxers before I wrapped my hand around my cock.

Holy fucking shit.

I didn't realize my eyes were closed until I had to pry them open. Joshua was watching me with wide, hungry eyes—he looked shocked and desperate and was not blinking as he watched my hand move beneath my boxers.

I could hear how loud I was breathing but couldn't care. My precum mixed with Joshua's as I stroked myself firm and hard, already feeling that fire building too high in my stomach.

Joshua slowly slid off the bed and his knees hit the floor. He ran his hands across my shoulders and down my chest, before settling at my hips and slowly, gently pulling my boxers down to my knees, the material stretched tight. My fist stumbled a little but quickly picked up the pace now that there was nothing in the way.

"Oh, Joshua, Josh, fuck, Josh, yeah," I was babbling, but too far gone to be embarrassed. His eyes were pitch black and he licked his hand again and again until his spit was dripping. I watched him, feeling a whine in the back of my throat. *Fuck, that's hot. Fuck, fuck.* Then Joshua's hand fell to my cock and he started to move in earnest, both of our hands moving and working. When it got to be too much, my hand lowered to my balls, the feeling causing a breathless tightening in my chest and gut, Joshua's hand not breaking at all in its punishing fucking, and then I was crying out and Joshua had crashed his lips to mine, swallowing my moans as I broke, spilling over his fist and fingers like he had for me just moments before.

His hands and lips moved slower and softer as I came down from my high. He was peppering light kisses against my cheeks and lips and forehead, and when I opened my eyes again to see him staring at me with a bright wonder, he kissed me gently. I kissed back, spent.

Quietly, Joshua grabbed my discarded boxers and helped clean us both up and then pulled me into bed. He didn't say anything and neither did I, but we didn't have to. Unlike the first night we'd spent together, this time Joshua was leaning into me, curled into my chest. His cheek was pressed to me, one arm thrown around me. Though he held himself tight, when I lifted a hand to stroke his hair, he relaxed into me, trusting me to take care of him as he did earlier.

My chest felt so full, my body so relaxed, that I was falling asleep in minutes with only one thought in my mind: I was so, so happy to be alive.

Chapter 16 - *Joshua*

The next morning, I woke up before Jay. I wondered if he was a heavy sleeper. Both times I'd spent the night, he'd been passed out long after I woke up.

This time, though, there would be no sneaking out. I rolled onto my side, the couch bed squeaking a little at the effort, and watched him sleep.

Jay looked younger in his sleep. He had a bit of stubble back, not a lot, but a light shadow cast over his jaw. His eyelashes were long—they curled against his cheeks, his lips parted just lightly. He was handsome, which I already knew, but looking at him like this, I was distinctly aware of how *pretty* he was, too.

I didn't know how long I stayed like that, but eventually, my stomach was growling and Jay was showing absolutely no signs of waking up. I wondered if that had something to do with being a trucker—sleep a lot when you can, build it up. I didn't know. I glanced around but there were no clocks out and my cell phone was—hell, probably still in my car.

Slowly, I unwound myself from the sheets and blankets. While standing above Jay, I couldn't help but feel a sense of contentment. Last night had been a bit of a whirlwind emotionally. Hell, the whole day had been. But now it was over and I felt—good.

I shook my head. I was being unnecessarily sappy. I found the loaned sweatpants that Jay had given me and looked around. There was no paper or pen for me to leave a note. I tiptoed into the garage where the dryer was. My clothes were all dry, if not a little cool from being outside, and I grabbed them quickly, changing into my own clothes before quietly leaving out the garage door.

Jay's place was close enough to the bakery that, after grabbing my wallet and phone from the car, I just walked the few blocks over. Hopefully, my time away would be enough to wake Jay up. I shot him a quick text, hoping he'd check his phone before believing I was just dipping out again, and promised to bring back breakfast.

The weather was really nice—it was not even eight in the morning, and the sun was up but not too warm yet. I reveled in it, walking slowly so that I could spend as much time in it as possible. I was getting used to the clothes-sticking-hair-sopping heat, but it was nice to feel the breeze today.

The bakery's door was propped open, the windows too, and I could tell by the cheery voices inside that everyone was equally as enthralled with the great weather as me.

"Back again?" the woman behind the counter said.

I started—I hadn't expected her to recognize me. I'd been in twice now but it wasn't like this was *that* small of town.

People here, though—excluding my biological family, apparently—were really nice. I was starting to get used to it, even if it did leave me feeling a little rubbed raw.

"Can't help it. Best coffee in town." I didn't know that for sure, but the woman's face brightened and I was glad I'd said it.

"Two blacks?" she guessed.

I grinned. "And two—no, four, please—of whatever your best-selling baked goods are. I don't really know what to choose."

I went over to look at the cakes in the display, marveling at how pretty they were. A sign declared them fresh baked daily. It was only eight in the morning—how had she baked all these cakes *and* the pastries? I imagined an army of bakers in the back, elbowing each other to get to the flour sifter.

I was laughing quietly at my own joke when someone tapped me on the shoulder. I turned around, jumping and smiling ruefully at the man I front of me.

"Jumpy," I said, shrugging.

The guy was tall, with dark hair and really bright green eyes. He swept his hair out of his eyes, smiling politely at me. He was shifting, just a little, on the balls of his feet. "Uh, sorry to bother you. I'm Alexander. Benson. Alexander Benson. I, uh. My family has a pretty big farm outside of town. Sort of a stable. But, guess you wouldn't know it. Not from here. But. Anyway. You're, um, Josh, right?"

"Joshua," I corrected, nodding. "Uh, hey."

"So, I just—wanted to ask. How'd it go with the Selwyns?"

My eyes widened. "Damn. News travel fast here."

Alexander laughed. "You got that right."

"Uh, yeah. What, uh, do you know?" I was a little nervous about my personal business being all over the town. With the vehement rejection that the family offered, I wouldn't have thought they'd be sharing all that much.

Then I remembered that random woman sitting in the living room with us. Dang.

"There's a rumor that you're related to them?"

"Uh, yeah. I mean, sort of. Yeah, there's a DNA match that confirmed Luke and I, at least, are siblings."

He took a step back, smiling wide. "Uh, wow. Okay, so, I'm—I have two brothers. I mean, we're not in the DNA system, but we're *also* biological siblings with Luke—so, uh, we'd probably be biological brothers to you, too."

"Shit," I breathed out, feeling surprised. "I—didn't think there'd be anyone else."

Alexander shrugged a little. "Listen, I know you weren't looking for this, but, uh—we'd love to get to know you. If you wanted."

I didn't know what to say.

"Two black coffees and a pastry arrangement," the woman at the counter called over to me.

I jumped, looking between the counter and the woman. "Uh, thanks." I went over and collected the cupholder and bag, handing the woman a twenty-dollar bill.

"Here," Alexander came over and grabbed a pen off the counter, scribbling a number on a napkin. He shoved it between the two large cups. "Call if you want. I'm—we'd like to, you know, get to know you. If you want."

I nodded. "Uh, for sure. Thanks."

I left, tucking the bag on the drink tray, moving slowly through the streets. Part of it was to appreciate the weather and not spill the breakfast I'd gathered, but mostly to contemplate what Alex had said.

Calling Alex meant meeting my brothers. Brothers. Not just one but multiple. A family.

My chest felt heavy.

Calling Alex, meeting my brothers, meant—well, it meant accepting that I did have family. Not the family I knew but a family, my family, and potentially family that wanted me to be theirs, too.

That wasn't the kind of thing that happened in one afternoon though. That was—more. It had to be more. If I called Alex, I couldn't just have lunch one day and go back to Kentucky the next. If I had been rejected by them, the way I was with the Selwyns, well, yeah. No point in staying.

But the opportunity for brothers? It meant, well. It meant I had to really try. I'd have to stay. At least for a little while.

Was that even what I wanted though? Should I stay? Could I stick around? One brother didn't want me—but there were *three* that might. That was a hell of a lot better deal than what I thought when I came here.

It wasn't like I had any reason *not* to stay. I didn't have a job or an apartment or anything that was pulling me back to Kentucky. If I stayed here, I could, I don't know—build something. Something that was all mine. Some of the people here were nice and some of them were family and wasn't that a good of enough reason to at least *consider* sticking around?

A small, hopeless part of me was whispering that staying here meant staying near Jay, at least until he sold the house.

I got back faster than I wanted, creaking open the door. Jay was in the kitchen and he jumped when I walked in.

He grinned sheepishly. "Startled me."

"Sorry," I said, kicking the door closed behind me gently. I lifted the tray in the air. "Brought breakfast."

He set the empty coffee pot down, his smile widening. "Just about to make some."

"This is better," I said, setting it on the counter.

Jay was in a pair of boxers and a white t-shirt, his bathrobe open. "Those from Mountain Bakery?"

"Yep!" I tore open the paper bag, turning it into a makeshift plate. There were two different scones, one looked like a turnover, and a big Danish. "Take your pick."

He reached out.

"Wait!" He froze. "Are you allergic? Shit, I didn't even think to ask."

He smiled at me kindly and grabbed what looked like an almond scone. He took a big bite. "Just cats," he mumbled around a mouthful.

I rolled my eyes and grabbed the turnover, taking a bite. "Fuck, that's good."

He laughed, the sound a little startled.

"Good morning?" he asked.

I shrugged. "Interesting morning," I clarified. He tilted his head but didn't ask. He was good like that, not prying. A sudden thought pushed its way into my head. What would it mean, staying here? Jay and I were supposed to be a casual fling. Something unimportantly casual. If I stayed here, would that change things? I didn't know I could take that. I knew that he mattered to me, but still, we were only meant to be a fling.

I took a sip of the coffee, wincing at the heat, and took the lid off so it would cool. Seeing me, Jay set his own lid aside.

"Jay," I said, tearing at the turnover and popping a small piece in my mouth. I chewed slowly, building up nerve to bring up heavy things at breakfast.

I could maybe commit to brothers. But I couldn't commit to anything else. Too many roots meant that when they inevitably got torn out, I would be torn, too. My hands shook just thinking about it.

I couldn't handle more.

Still. The hammering in my chest wasn't just fear of more. It was also fear of less.

"We're just—this isn't serious, right? I just need to clarify, like, this is just a fling."

I felt suspended in mid-air. What would Jay say? If we were just a fling, I could stay. That would be okay. But I thought that a part of me, growing bigger with every passing second, every beating of my heart, would be devastated.

If he said we were more, that part of me would be elated. But I'd probably have to run back to Griff and my friends as fast as my legs could take me.

I was a jumbled mess of contradictions and I knew of no way to convey this to Jay.

Jay's eyes widened in surprise and he slowly lowered the scone from his parted lips. He set it down, following the movement with his eyes, before looking up at me. "Yeah. Of course. Just a fling."

Disappointment flared, sinking low in my gut, and I tried to swallow past it. I took a long pull of my coffee to hide my expression, ignoring how hot it was. "Right. That's what I thought."

He was tearing the scone apart with his fingertips. When he noticed me watching him, he popped a bit of it in his mouth.

This was a good thing—I didn't want him to want more because *I* didn't want more. I couldn't have more. People didn't stick around. I knew that. I couldn't stick to anyone, either.

It just—sort of stung, is all. But it was early and I needed caffeine and it was probably just from still being emotionally raw from yesterday. I didn't want anything real with him.

Right?

Chapter 17 - *Jay*

Joshua didn't say anything else as we finished our breakfast, outside of offering me the last bite of the Danish. He didn't look *upset* necessarily; just like he was disappointed. Maybe he had wanted the almond scone. I should have asked.

I drank the last of my coffee. Joshua was fiddling with his cup.

He was quiet, which wasn't necessarily unusual—I was quiet enough that Joshua often took my lead. But now, the quiet was *different*.

Had I upset him somehow last night? I hadn't meant to. I knew that I had played with him a little last night, waiting until he had asked for it before giving him anything, knew that he had been writhing and desperate—but he hadn't seemed upset. He had seemed like he'd liked it.

I wanted him to see that I wanted him—that he was wanted, but also that I would wait for his lead. That he could set whatever boundaries he wanted or ask for anything and I would follow it.

Maybe it was too subtle. Maybe sex wasn't the best way to deliver that type of message.

Still—he liked it when we had sex. I knew that much.

With the half-assed form of a plan in mind, I reached over and took Joshua's hand in mine. He frowned a little, but more in confusion than dislike, and led him to the bed that I hadn't bothered making yet. He smiled at me, a little bit indulgently, and toed off his boots.

"Jeans, too," I ordered.

He lifted an eyebrow but complied, shimmying out and then settling on the bed, his ankles crossed. "Good?"

"Good," I agreed, smiling. I slid out of my bathrobe and settled on the bed next to him.

"Why am I here?" he asked, gesturing to the bed.

I purposefully misunderstood. Reaching over, I wound one hand in his hair and my thumb stroked gently at the spot below his ear. "On Earth?"

He was nuzzling a little into my hand. "No," he said, after a beat. I grinned at him. His eyes had fallen closed and he was leaning into my touch. "On the bed."

"Oh, that." I leaned forward and kissed him once softly before pulling away.

His eyes opened and his expression, though no less conflicted, was more vulnerable than I had seen it.

I didn't know what happened this morning that had Joshua looking like this—if it was my fault, or someone else's. All I knew was that I *hated* it. My chest hurt looking at it, and I couldn't think of anything to say.

So I didn't say anything. I just kissed him again. This time, he kissed me back.

We kissed softly, lowering ourselves so we were lying on our sides. Joshua's hands were around my wrists, holding me in place next to him as we explored each other's mouths.

We had kissed before, of course—had done much more than that, too. But this was different.

I moved my mouth to his neck, kissing and drawing short little gasps from him. It was softer, slower, than we had been the other nights. I kissed him to taste his skin, to feel his goosebumps rise and bump against my tongue, to find where I had to kiss to make his fingers tighten their grip and where he relaxed.

He was a mystery, no matter how many times I had had him.

I tugged on the bottom of his t-shirt, asking permission. Joshua replied by rolling over and stripping it off himself, then coming back to recapture my lips. We undressed each other the rest of the way quickly, until our bodies were pressed tight against each other.

He was hard against my thigh, his cock firm but not insistent as we continued to kiss. Joshua would offer his neck to me and I would kiss and lick every bit, while his hands would gently explore my back. Then he would nudge me away and kiss softly at my own neck, and then trailed down my chest, tongue swirling around my nipples and down to my hip bones. He was slow, purposeful, in his every kiss, his hands smoothing down the planes of my body as his fingertips gently had me shivering. By the time his fingers made it to my thighs, I was growing hard, heat swelling in my stomach.

His fingertips gently trailed up and down my cock. I was growing harder and harder under his gentle, slow touch.

When I was fully hard, he reached up, hands framing my face as he kissed me. It was slow and deep, no fight. He hitched one leg over my waist and I tugged him closer. Our bodies pressed tightly against each other.

"Do you have anything?" he asked, pressing his face to my neck. The words were muffled but punctuated by a kiss.

I sighed happily, his mouthing at my neck making my whole body fall relaxed. He slowly started to rotate his hips, cock catching on mine and we both let out a low hiss.

"Condom," he said, more forcefully this time.

I didn't have to be told a *third* time, then.

I unraveled myself from him and grabbed the lube and condom from my bag as quickly as I could. When I rejoined him in bed, his hands reached for me greedily, pulling me down to him. He kissed me as if I had been gone more than just a few seconds.

He reached for the lube but this time I kept it, pouring a generous amount out on my fingers, and then reaching between us. His legs fell open, feet planted on the bed and knees high so I could reach beneath him.

I opened him up slowly, but not for long. He had turned, his face pressing hard into the pillow, hips rotating, and his cock was bobbing up and down on his stomach. I pulled away, dropping a light kiss on the head and he gasped, jerking up. He glared at me half-heartedly and I grinned.

Joshua reached beside me and grabbed the condom, tearing it open and slowly rolling it onto me. I had to grit my teeth to keep from groaning and he grinned at me. *Revenge,* his eyes were saying.

I'd glare but it felt too good. When the condom was on, he poured more lube on it, rubbing gently.

When I was ready, I lifted Joshua's leg and slid in slowly.

He let out a gasped *"Fuck, Jay!"* And I couldn't stop the shaking moan.

It was slow, a little tender, his legs curling around my waist. His hands were above his head, fists in the sheets, and I reached up a hand and curled my fingers around his wrist, holding him in place. His back arched just a little, eyes flying to me. I leaned down and kissed him. He kissed back, relaxing underneath my ministrations.

My hips rotated slowly. I had to focus a little carefully at not just hammering into him—his tight heat was dizzying, and my body was shaking with the effort.

Joshua's upper body was twisting, his hips reaching to meet me. Though it was slow, it wasn't any less intense—there was something desperate in the way our bodies were coming together, his eyes clenched shut, sweat from my chest dripping onto his. His legs were tight around me, holding me as close as he could.

His hands were flexing and when I let go, my hips snapping up to meet his, his hands flew to my face and he yanked me down in a harsh kiss.

While the heat was climbing in me, my stomach clenching and my head dizzy from how good as it was, there was something—different about the way that Joshua was clinging to me.

There was something a little unraveled in my chest—something that was desperate for me to close the incredibly small space between Joshua and I, something that was saying any amount of space was too much. I didn't know what to do with it—I had *just* told him that I was all right with this being just a fling. It was what *he* wanted.

But what he wanted, what we should want, was very different than the sharp need in my chest.

He kissed me, arms around my neck and holding me close. His hips were rotating in small circles and I could feel the pressure building and building.

When I came, Joshua pulled away from my mouth, his head falling to my shoulders and his hands clinging to me. I let my hips snap harder than they had been, once, twice, three times as I spilled into him and when I let out a low moan, his name warbled in the breath, he came, untouched, between us.

Heart hammering, we untangled and cleaned off quickly, quietly. Joshua returned to my arms as soon as he could and while I held him, I tried to figure out what the hell I was feeling.

There was some sort of automatic happiness at having Joshua in my arms—I could feel that, settling like warmth in my chest. But there was also something hollow in my gut, something like homesickness even as I lay in my own childhood home, the only home I had ever known.

I didn't understand it. Joshua was leaning against me like maybe he was just as conflicted.

"How was your day yesterday?" Joshua said after a few minutes of silence.

I shrugged and then bit the inside of my cheek. He was trying to talk to me. I should at least meet him halfway. "I had a buyer interested yesterday. They came by and looked at the place, seems like it might work out without all that work."

Joshua was quiet. Then after a full minute. "And then you'll leave?"

"Maybe," I said, then frowned. "I mean, yeah. I've got to get back to work eventually, after all."

"Right."

"Not sure they'll bite, though. Realtor thought there were going to be a lot of fixes to make at first, so I don't really know if they'll want such a—a—"

"Fixer-upper?"

"Yeah," I nodded. "You should have heard them. They were talking about all the things they were going to change. Completely gut the bathroom."

"Needs it," Joshua commented. "It's a little outdated."

"I guess." He was right, of course. "Still don't like it, though."

Joshua pulled away and I only just stopped myself from protesting. He had one eyebrow raised. "It seems to me like you might not be as ready to let it go as you say you are."

I frowned, tilting my head. "The hell is that supposed to mean?"

Joshua shrugged and was saved by the ringing of my cell phone. I scrunched my nose at the sound. I slid out of bed, grabbing my robe and slipping it on. I padded into the kitchen and answered quickly.

It was Sarah Larson. The prospective buyers wanted to look at the house again with their realtor.

"So soon?" I glanced back in at Joshua. He was lying on the bed with his ankles crossed, arms folded behind his head as he watched me openly.

"When the buyers are *really interested,* these things can move very quickly," she said, sounding thrilled.

I frowned. "When?"

"Thirty minutes?" she said, tone lifting at the end to phrase it as a question.

I pulled the phone away to glance at the time and then back to Joshua. "All right. Thanks, Sarah."

"Thank you, Mr. Richardson!"

We hung up and I sighed. "Gotta go."

"What?" That had Joshua hopping up. I cleaned the kitchen quickly, throwing away our breakfast remnants.

"Can you get dressed?" I asked offhandedly. I was already searching for my clothes—my boxers were gross and so was the sleep shirt I had been wearing when Joshua arrived last night. I dug around in my duffel until I found clean clothes. I stepped into my boxers and glanced over at Joshua who was still naked. "Josh?"

"Right," he said, shaking his head as if to clear it. We both dressed quickly. I felt a little bad rushing him, but it took nearly twenty-five minutes to get fully ready, the bed packed away and our dirty linens in the wash. I slipped out with just a few minutes to go, ushering Josh out, too.

After locking up, I turned to see if Joshua wanted to continue our morning elsewhere, but he was already at his car climbing in. I waved and he nodded back.

My heart was beating fast, the morning a rush that had my pulse elevated. I wanted to ask Joshua how he felt. I wanted to crawl back into bed. I wanted—something that I couldn't quite put my finger on.

I watched as his car peeled out of the neighborhood. I had the distinct feeling like I had fucked up and had no goddamn idea how.

Chapter 18 - *Joshua*

I wasn't angry that Jay needed me to go; it was fine, it made sense. I had to get out so that he could show the house. He had to show the house because he wanted to sell the house. He wanted to sell the house and then he would leave and—

I was *upset* that he was leaving.

Which, fucking hell, *I* was leaving! This was ridiculous.

I was getting invested in a way that I never intended. I needed to take a step back.

This trip was about finding family—my biological family and I was just getting in over my head with this fling. Jay had made it clear what he wanted, which was nothing serious, just a fling. And that's what I wanted, too. It wasn't like I had gone and caught feelings.

Right?

I pushed the thought out of my mind, driving aimlessly for a while. I needed to harden my heart. I didn't want to stop seeing him while we were both here. He was *nice* and it was fun and I could handle no-strings-attached casual. It's what I always had. I could handle it—I just needed to harden my heart a little.

I needed to get back on track. I was here for family. So far, two dead-ends. The Selwyns were non-starters. They either were too far gone to recognize me or too unwilling to acknowledge me. But apparently, that wasn't my only option here in Bennett Wood.

I pulled over in a parking lot off the main road in town and took out my cellphone. The crumpled napkin from this morning was crinkled in my pocket and I pulled it out, smoothing it out enough to read the numbers.

I texted Alexander, biting on the edge of my thumbnail while I waited for it to go through. Almost immediately three little text bubbles popped up.

Hey! Awesome. We're at home on the farm. Wanna come here?

I glanced at the clock. It was early, but if he was asking, it probably wasn't too early for a visit. Nerves pulled at my stomach.

I texted back a quick, short *yes.*

He sent back a dropped location and I quickly plugged the phone into the aux cord, letting the GPS drive me through the winding roads of Bennett Wood.

The drive only took about ten minutes and then I was pulling off onto Swallow Drive.

The driveway was long but the house was huge, visible even from the road. Big and white, it looked like it belonged more in a movie set than in the back woods of this old town.

I parked next to a truck and took a deep breath.

Come on, Matthews. You got this.

I texted Alexander that I was there, though I was sure he knew, and slowly got out of the car. I took my time packing my cell and keys in my pockets, then stretching long and hard to rid my body of cricks. I could see Alexander on the porch, bouncing on the balls of his feet and looking around.

"Joshua! Hey!" Alexander jogged down the steps when I approached and skidded to a stop in front of me. Though it was a warm summer day and he was dressed in all black, he still had a happy, childlike grin and seemed excited by my presence.

"Hey, Alexander." I shoved my hands in my pockets for lack of better thing to do with them.

"Want a tour?" he asked, gesturing around him.

I shrugged and then decided that was rude. "Uh, yes, please."

He laughed lightly and smiled. "Come on."

"There are thirty acres," he started as we walked around the big house. "The house itself has— uh, five—yeah, five, bedrooms. Then there, that's the stable. Ten-horse stable. Dad used to have a lot more but we just have the three now. Do you ride horses?"

I had in summer camp once. It went terribly. "Not really."

Alexander waved it off, though he looked a little disappointed. "Anyway, we have the gardens and keep four cows and a bull. The farm's some income for Mom but it's also a giant hobby for some of us."

"You?"

He sent me a sideways look. "If Mom is looking."

I laughed. Alexander led me around the rest of property, giving a bit of a background to the history of the place. I peeked in on the horses but they were eating and there was no way in *hell* I was getting between those teeth and their next meal, even if Alexander was insistent that it would be okay.

The whole tour took maybe a half hour and then we were walking back to the house. He took the porch steps two at a time.

I followed him into the house hesitantly. I toed off my shoes when he did.

"Come on," he said, moving through the house quickly. I scrambled to catch up, not wanting to get lost in this thing. "Thirsty?"

"Sure," I said.

Alexander led me into a large kitchen. It was beautiful—bright and airy, with big windows and white granite countertops. He gestured to the breakfast bar and obediently I went and sat. He poured us glasses of sweet tea and I thanked him.

There was a clamoring outside of the kitchen and then two men came into the room.

They looked exactly like Alexander.

I glanced at him in surprise.

He was glaring at his brothers and when he noticed me, his expression turned sheepish. "Did I not mention my brothers were here?"

"You didn't mention you were identical. How many of there *are* you?"

One of the new Alexanders snorted. He was wearing a green Henley. "Just the three of us, unfortunately." He hopped onto the counter and held out his hand. "I'm Sean. That's Victor. He's the asshole."

The third brother, Victor, rolled his eyes. "He means oldest."

Alexander laughed. "Same diff." He poured two more glasses of tea and handed them to his brothers.

"So you're the mysterious Josh?"

"Joshua," I said.

Sean narrowed his eyes. "No nicknames among *brothers*?"

"My parents named me Joshua," I explained, fidgeting a little.

They didn't pry but I assumed at least *some* of my tragic backstory had made it from Hanna's mouth when she left the Selwyns' that day.

"Fine. Mysterious Joshua, then."

"That's me." I was glad they dropped it. I regretted my comment immediately.

"Mom is gonna want to meet you." Victor said, rapping his knuckles on the table. "I'll go get her."

My eyes widened and I looked to Alexander in panic. "Uh, your mom?"

If these were my brothers—what was this woman to me?

"Of course, our mom," Sean rolled his eyes.

I bit my lip. Victor shot his brother a glare.

While their silent conversation went on, I turned to Alex. "So, um. You weren't on my DNA test. How did you guys find out?"

The brothers quieted, all sharing another silent exchange. I fought back a bit of jealousy.

"We actually always knew. Our dad, Nels, he was infertile. So that was, like, how they had us. But we always knew our dad was our dad, no matter what some test said," Alex explained.

Sean snorted. "Course, we would've been more upset if we had known we weren't so special."

"Shut up, Sean," Victor groaned.

I thought about how different things would be if I had always known. Would've come here after the accident, instead of into the foster system, for one. I got lost imagining a childhood I'd never have, only barely managing to keep my attention focused on the brothers. Sean and Alexander were talking about some party and I tried to pay polite attention.

"You can come, you know. If you're gonna be in town."

"Oh," I was surprised. "Uh, yeah, maybe."

"Are you?"

Victor was back, along with a thin, blonde woman in a floral dress and—

"Maggie!" I couldn't hide the surprise or the delight.

She seemed just as surprised. "Joshua!"

"What are *you* doing here?" I couldn't help the question spilling out.

"I *do* have friends, you know. I'm not too old for that."

I laughed and apologized. Maggie winked at me.

The blonde woman, the triplets' mom, looked between us in surprise. "You know our guest, Maggie?"

Maggie was in a long brown shawl and had her gray hair pinned up elaborately. She was an enigma and I was thankful for her slightly familiar presence.

"Ah, we're acquainted." She winked at me. "Visited me in my museum. How'd it go with your, uh, friend?"

I could feel my cheeks flush. "Uh, well, thank you."

She laughed. Sean joined in, apparently sensing from my blush that whatever she was saying was embarrassing.

"Seems quite unfair, that everyone knows Joshua but me," the woman said, elbowing her son pointedly. I liked her immediately.

"Mom," Victor said, rolling his eyes. "This is Joshua—uh."

"Matthews," I supplied.

"Joshua Matthews. Joshua, this is our mother, Georgia Benson."

"So nice to meet you, Josh."

"Joshua," the triplets all corrected in unison.

"Joshua, then," she smiled kindly.

"Um, hi, ma'am."

Her face froze and Victor and Sean started laughing. "Uh uh. No. No ma'am. Georgia, please, honey."

"Sorry, Georgia." I was sure I was bright red now. Alexander, at least, had the decency to not laugh at me, even if he was looking just as amused as his brothers.

"*Anyway,*" Sean said pointedly, staring at his brother. Maggie and Georgia took a seat on either side of me at the bar and Victor went to lean against the cabinets. "Are you?"

Everyone turned to look at me. "Uh. What?"

"Is he what?" Georgia asked, a little impatiently. I was grateful to her.

Sean turned to his mom. "Sticking around in town."

All heads turned again.

I tried not to fidget. I failed.

"Uh, I'm not sure, honestly. I just sort of—came here, you know. I don't have a place to live or a job lined up."

"So you could stay," Alexander said, sounding a little eager. "Theoretically."

"Yeah, yeah," I said, nodding. "I guess—yeah, I could. I need to find work anyway, you know, before my cash runs out."

"What do you like to do?" Georgia asked.

I bit down on my lip, thinking. "I—don't have *much* experience. I just graduated this spring, with, um, marketing and public relations? I really like—just, liking things. Does that make sense?"

"That does," she said kindly. She reached over and took the tea out of Sean's hand. He protested lightly but stopped when she took a sip. "You know, that *does* remind me, Maggie."

The woman was already smirking knowingly. "Yes, Georgia?"

"You've been complaining quite frequently about your lack of help at the museum."

Hope along with embarrassment warred in my chest.

"I suppose," Maggie was squinting her eyes, lips pursed.

"Surely you could give the young man an interview, assuming your schedule permits that? It would be—beneficial."

Maggie laughed, no longer able to hold it in. "Oh, shush, Georgia. You'll have an aneurysm with that scheming."

Georgia took another sip of the tea, winking at Alexander. Maggie turned to me.

"How's Monday at noon?"

My jaw dropped. "Uh," I looked between the others. Alexander was nodding emphatically. Sean gave me a thumbs-up. "Sure."

"Bring lunch. I like onion rings."

I grinned wide. "Yes, ma'am."

For the first time, in a place that I had never been before, I felt completely at ease. There was something distinctly *right* about this place.

I glanced at the brothers—shit, at *my* brothers—and they were all grinning, too.

Well. Here goes nothing.

Chapter 19 - *Jay*

The offer was put in on the house by noon.

It was less than what I had hoped for, but Sarah assured me that was because I hadn't had to pay for the changes in the house or any of the work we had talked about. It was still a good amount—enough for me to buy a new place, somewhere else, to start to settle down.

The offer was good and immediate, just like I had been hoping.

But still, I had told Sarah I would call her back by tomorrow. I needed some *time* to consider.

When she had asked, bewildered, what I needed to consider, I had just said goodbye and hung up.

Something felt *wrong.* It wasn't the number, really, and it wasn't the people. It was just— something in my gut was telling me that this was a bad idea.

It sounded a lot like Joshua's voice.

"It seems to me like you might not be as ready to let it go as you say you are."

That's what Joshua had said. That I wasn't as ready to let go as I said I was.

Wasn't I ready to let go? The whole house, besides the garage, was packed. I had donated most of Mom's things. I was selling the house—it wasn't like Mom would be upset. We had talked about this before she passed. It was—it was fine. It was the plan.

But why did the plan suddenly feel like a huge mistake?

I made a pot of coffee, pacing around the kitchen as I waited for it to brew.

"You might not be as ready to let it go as you say you are."

I imagined what would happen if I *didn't* sell the house.

I'd keep it. There were some changes that Sarah had recommended that maybe should be done. I could see the benefit. Not the beams in the bedroom, because, come *on*. But the updated bathroom could be good. It was too small for me anyway, had been since I was sixteen.

A fresh coat of paint. No more wallpaper.

I imagined the house updated, adjusted—the same good, strong bones, the same layout, but just a little more—me.

I imagined living here. Getting groceries and coming home, cooking. I imagined Joshua at the kitchen table, laughing at me while I fried burgers or made lasagna or any other unnecessarily sappy domestic task I could think of.

Joshua was just passing by, but maybe he could stick around—for a little bit. After all, he said he'd help with the work on the house. I could thank him for the work with food and with affection and then maybe a few weeks, a few months from now—

I shook my head.

Fuck, what was I thinking?

The coffee spluttered. I poured a mug and rubbed my temples. A headache was coming on and I knew there was no way to shake it—at least not until I made a decision.

It was a *good* offer. It was what I wanted.

Wasn't it?

I drank my coffee slowly, trying to clear my head. I refilled the mug and went to the garage. I needed to pack the rest of the stuff—it was all mostly put away out there, just needed shifting between what I would keep and donate.

The first few boxes were mostly old clothes that Mom had written "Donate" on, probably a half-dozen years ago at this point. I pushed them to the edge of the garage and kept sifting.

There were a few boxes of my old junk, stuff that she had moved when my room got repurposed after I didn't come home for enough years. Flashes of guilt niggled at the edge of my head, and I tried to ignore it. Mom understood. We did talk and we did see each other—just not here, not that often.

I moved all that stuff to donate. If I didn't miss it once in the last twenty years, I doubted I'd start missing it now.

I had gotten to the bottom of the boxes, all labeled with various holidays. I didn't need to keep the decorations, really—where would I put them? In the rig of the truck? I snorted. That would be a sight.

Still, I opened the boxes, curiosity taking over.

The first one, a Thanksgiving one, had dusty paper turkeys, old arts and crafts from my grade school projects, place settings and tablecloths. I moved those to the side.

In the next one, I moved more slowly through the items. The first of the Christmas boxes were all ornaments. I held each one, remembering when Mom and I would decorate the tree each year. Mom loved holidays. We would handmake a new ornament together every year. Even when I was old enough to think it was lame and embarrassing, we would still be together on Christmas Eve, painting some new bauble.

Something not quite guilt but not quite sorrow was building in my chest. I swallowed hard and set that box aside. I would be keeping this one then.

I opened the next and there were a few more ornaments, Mom's old Nativity scene, and a large, hand-painted blue jay.

Slowly, I pulled the blue jay out. It was plastic, unlike her typical favoring of glass figurines. I squinted at it, using my flannel to wipe any dust off of it. It was familiar, I just couldn't put my finger on why.

I moved it around to look at the back and when I did, the middle popped open. I blinked in surprise, first afraid that I had broken the fragile thing, before I realized it was actually a capsule.

Suddenly, I remembered it.

Mom had given it to me on the first day of high school. I had been fourteen, closeted, terrified, and desperately unwilling to participate in my mom's dorky traditions. So she had made all new ones. This one only lasted the one year, though—writing down all my future ambitions so I could work toward them for the year.

I was careful with the paper. It was old, yellowed with age, and I was afraid my hands would force disintegration.

It was my handwriting, if not a little clumsier. Thick black print, still legible.

There were a dozen different wishes. Hopes. Things I had once wanted enough to write down, hope for. I could barely remember any of them.

I wanted to have a family—it said it, right there. Wife and kids. I snorted. *Sorry, kid,* I thought. *You're not getting that one. Not exactly, at least.*

I wanted to build a tree house in the back yard that no one else could go in, not without my invite. Mom and I had bought the wood but I had given up. I wondered if it was still out back, in the shed.

I wanted to be the mayor of Bennett Wood.

I wanted to buy a house down the road from Mom.

I wanted a lot of things back when I was a kid that I hadn't even remembered. These were my *dreams.* Where had they all gone?

If the kid I was back then could see me now, he would be disappointed. Forty-eight, alone, a good job but no home or family to come back to, Bennett Wood so far in my rearview I had even forgotten about him.

I gently refolded the paper, placing it back in the blue jay capsule. I moved the whole box to the keep pile.

I didn't believe in signs much. I never had. Life was what we made out of it—letting fate in was a fool's errand.

But my mom believed in signs. In particular, she believed in blue jays.

I knew what she would say if she was here. My reluctance to sell, my desire for roots, that *feeling* in my chest when Joshua was around—and now this blue jay-shaped reminder that even though I had run from this place when I was a kid, it was still my home. Always my home. I had been too afraid, thinking it wouldn't accept me. I had never considered that it already had.

I groaned, burying my face in my hands. When I looked up, on top of the bookshelf that I hadn't yet cleaned, was the little ceramic blue jay I had stopped Josh from packing. It's painted eyes were boring straight in mine.

I held my breath for so long that it almost hurt to let it go.

I almost laughed. "All right, Mom. I hear you."

Mom believed in fate and blue jays. I guess it was about time I tried to, too.

Chapter 20 - *Joshua*

Sitting on the log by the fire pit, I stared into the ash. I hadn't bothered lighting it, but I wasn't ready to crawl into my tent yet. I had spent the entire afternoon at the Benson farm, getting to know my brothers.

It had been—different. But good. Good different, for sure. It was what I had hoped I would have gotten from Luke when I first came to Bennett Wood, except a bit better. Instead of one brother, I had three. Three that *actually* wanted to get to know me, wanted me to stay. I had that job interview on Monday—I had a job and a family and—

Well, there were still a few things up in the air.

Namely, Jay.

I couldn't get him out of my head. Earlier, when I had left the farm, the first thing I had done was driven toward his house. I wanted to tell him—wanted him to know about Alexander and Sean and Victor, about how *nice* Georgia was, about how I saw Maggie again. I wanted to tell him that I wanted to stay in town and, fuck it, I wanted *him* to stay in town and I wanted to give this a real shot.

My heart hammered in my chest. The realization felt like a hammer over the head, even as it became so *obvious* as soon as I thought it.

I *liked* Jay. I really, really liked him and I knew that people could reject you, could leave you, but I wanted to give it a shot. Give Jay a shot.

I stood abruptly. The adrenaline was coursing through my body. It was now or never.

I was just at the campsite's parking lot when Jay's little beige car pulled in.

I froze, my keys half raised, as I watched him park next to me.

He scrambled out of the car and I watched him with my mouth half open in surprise.

"I've been looking for you," he said as he climbed out, slamming the door behind him. He moved quickly, but froze when he got to the other side of the car. His eyes flickered down to the keys in my hand. "Going somewhere?"

"No," I said quickly, ignoring the heat in my cheeks and ears. I shoved my keys in my pocket. "Uh, what—" I cleared my throat. "What are you doing here?"

"Looking for you," Jay said, as if it was obvious. There was only a little bit of room between our two cars—he had parked right next to me. The lot was empty beside us.

"I was coming to look for you, too." I admitted.

Jay's eyes widened. "You—were?"

"Yes," I said, nodding. My tongue darted out of my mouth nervously, licking my bottom lip. Jay's eyes traced the movement.

"I—okay. I have—okay." He stopped, and then started again. "I know that we agreed on— this—" he gestured between us. "This was just a *fling,* something casual. I know that. And I will respect that, if that's what you want. I will. I just—I had to—tell you." He swallowed. "I have feelings for you. I have feelings for you and I want to see where this goes. I want it to be more than just a fling."

He sucked in a large breath, eyes wide as he held it. His cheeks were bright pink and he looked so *nervous.*

Jay was a man of just a few words. He was quiet and considerate of each syllable that came out. I imagined that it had taken a lot to say what he just had.

It took everything in me to stop from grabbing him by his dumb flannel and kissing him senseless.

Instead, I settled for nodding emphatically. "Yes, yes." I said, grinning. "I—yes, please."

Jay exhaled in a rush, his answering smiling brilliant and bright on his face. He swayed closer to me and I reached out, hands flying to his flannel. I held the material in my hands. His hands fell to my waist, and we held each other.

Jay's smile faded just a little, and a quick frown took over before he smoothed it out. "You were right. About—the house. I—I couldn't do it. I think I'm going to keep it. I'll fix it up, just a little, and I'll—just wait. I might just keep it."

I smiled. My hand reached up automatically and I hesitated, hand hovering. His eyes widened. I pushed past the feelings of nerves and brushed my knuckles against his cheek, and reached up to kiss him softly. He kissed me back just as tenderly.

"I'm happy for you," I said genuinely.

He blushed. "I—this means, I guess, we have to do long distance. If we're trying and I'm staying here. Or, you know. Um. You could, well…" he trailed off, hand dropping from my side. He nervously tugged on one of his ears.

I felt my grin grow. "Stay here? In Bennett Wood?"

He sucked in a quick breath and nodded.

I bumped his shoulder lightly. "I was actually already planning on it."

Jay's smile grew. "You were?"

"I was," I nodded.

Jay swayed closer. I wound my arms around his neck and he tilted his head lower. His lips found mine and we kissed. This time, there was no desperation, no indifference—just Jay and me and all the time in the world.

I didn't know how long we had kissed but when we pulled back, I was gasping for air and Jay's eyes were dark.

"Uh," I cleared my throat. "Now that we, uh, got the relationship status out of the way, does that mean we get to have celebration sex?"

Jay's eyes widened, eyebrows shooting to his hairline. "How is that different from regular sex?"

I grinned at him wickedly, tugging him closer. He stumbled and his hands shot out against my car to catch himself. "I'll just have to show you."

He swallowed hard. "Uh, yeah. That. Let's do that."

I grinned and kissed him lightly on the side of his throat. I felt him gulp. "Your place or mine?" I gestured toward the tent.

He laughed. His hand reached down and his fingers threaded through mine. He tugged me toward his car. "Come on, Josh. Let's go home."

I didn't mind the sound of that at all.

Epilogue - *Jay*

The June sun was beaming in from all the open doors and windows in the house. Though there was a light breeze, I was still sweating and the smell of wet paint was permeating the small house.

I had three and a half walls done with their first coat and was glaring angrily at the last. I was *tired.* Why had I decided that hiring painters was a bad idea? If I had hired people, they'd be done, my living room would be painted, and I'd be relaxing or doing something—good God, anything—else.

I groaned aloud. Joshua had warned me.

I lifted the paint roller again. Well, just because he was right didn't mean I wanted him to know that. I had to finish the room before he came home from work.

It had only been a few weeks since Joshua had decided to stick around, getting a job at the museum and trying to get to know his biological brothers better. I was selfishly thrilled. Although it had taken two days of arguing and at least three promises to pay rent, I had finally convinced him to take the second bedroom. We'd negotiated that he'd help with some of the work in lieu of rent. If we stuck to the plan, the house would be fully updated by the time the summer ended.

Josh had joked that it would be weird for boyfriends to be roommates. I hadn't been able to come up with a good retort, but I blamed that on it being the first time he'd called us boyfriends.

Smiling fondly at the memory, I dipped the roller in the paint and attacked the last wall.

I had just finished the first coat when Joshua came in.

"Honey, I'm home!" he joked. He did it every day and while at first I laughed, and then rolled my eyes, I admitted silently to myself that I was actually incredibly fond of the cheesy greeting.

"Hey." I set the roller down, lifting up my t-shirt to wipe the sweat on my forehead. Josh was grinning, leaning against the doorway as he watched me. I rolled my eyes. "Don't be a pervert."

"Can't help it," he teased.

I laughed. "Shut up. How was the museum?"

Joshua sighed, pushing off the wall. His expression fell and he came closer to me, wrapping his arms around my neck. "Luke was there."

Joshua's biological brother that didn't want anything to do with him. I winced and wrapped one arm around his waist. "I'm sorry."

"He was there with a few friends. Didn't say *anything* to me."

I nodded. "Still giving you a wide berth then."

"Yeah," he leaned his forehead on my shoulder. I dropped a small kiss on his ear and he shivered. I held him for a minute, letting him rest his body against mine. I knew it was hard on him. In a month, he'd gained three brothers, and an extra, complicated layer to his already pretty dramatic backstory—the real reason that he was related to the Selwyns.

Finding out that not only was Josh the brother of Luke, but the son of Dr. Selwyn, and that Dr. Selwyn had known all along was one big reveal; learning just *how* Dr. Selwyn had impregnated Josh's mom and how many women were involved, though, was a whole other thing altogether.

It had been a rough few weeks after that, Joshua trying to come to terms with the news that his birth mom had been nonconsensually inseminated. For two days, he hadn't even crawled out of bed. But things were better now—brighter every day, especially when he spent time with his brothers. I tried not to let it go to my head that he had confessed having me so steadfastly there for him had helped.

He was still a little quiet, especially about the things he was so insecure about. But as he grew more confident with his place with the brothers, the more he was opening up to me. I didn't mind having to wait. For Josh, I had all the time in the world.

Joshua pulled back and kissed my nose. I smiled at him. "Just give it some time. You know that, as hard as this all is for you and the triplets, it's gotta be hard on Luke."

Josh raised his eyebrows. "How mature."

"I am older than you," I joked.

He laughed. "You got that right."

I swatted at his shoulder lightly. "I'm sure Luke will come around once this all dies down."

Josh tilted his head, expression incredulous. "Does this kind of thing ever die down? The man had been using *his own sperm* on his fertility patients for years. I'm not the only random brother that Luke has."

There was a light thrum of guilt in his voice. I stamped on it immediately. "Don't go feeling guilty."

"I opened a whole can of worms," he complained.

"The doctor was *violating* people. Everyone deserves to know." Joshua nodded, but still looked conflicted. I sighed and pulled him to me again. "Besides. You know, it *did* bring us together, after all."

He laughed, the feeling vibrating against my chest. "Well, then it was definitely worth it." I could feel his smile against my bare collarbone.

He turned around, leaning against me. "Can't believe you got this whole room painted."

"Told you I would," I said, then added, lying, "It was easy."

He snorted, not believing me. "I like this color blue, Jay. It's pretty."

I looked around. The room was starting to come together—the whole house was. *I* was. "Yeah, I like it, too."

I held Josh in my arms. Even though the future was still unclear and everything was new, there was one thing I was certain of: this, right here, was right.

I looked down at Josh, his eyes drinking in the living room I was building for us, and I sent a little prayer of thanks to my mom and her blue jays.

Printed in Great Britain
by Amazon